"Laura Buzo's ability to write beneath the surface of seemingly ordinary lives makes [this book] stand out. . . . A deft character novel told through the witty voice of a teenage girl." —Australian Government Office for the Arts

"I loved it. Even when Chris drove me up the wall. Even when Amelia needed to buck her ideas. Because it made me all tingly and happy inside. . . . They made me want to scream and then smush them into a rather awkward group hug." —The Crooked Shelf (blog)

"This isn't your typical love story: it's honest, bittersweet, and insightful, with the characters lending you their lives to let you look into your own." —YA Reads (blog)

"This is a book that I immediately wanted to recommend to friends. Love and Other Perishable Items is realistic young adult fiction. So realistic, in fact, that it's sometimes a bit painful to read." —Jen Robinson's Book Page (blog)

"It's a great universal story about love, longing, and growing up. . . . One of my favorite reads of 2012." —Stacked (blog)

"Because I loved both Amelia and Chris. Because of capturing that wonderful feeling of longing for another. Because Chris's seeking something is just as achingly drawn. This is a **Favorite Book Read in 2013**." —A Chair, A Fireplace and a Tea Cozy (blog)

LOVE
and other perishable items

Laura Buzo

EMBER

Text copyright © 2010 by Laura Buzo
Cover art copyright © 2012 by Irene Lamprakou/Trevillion Images

All rights reserved. Published in the United States by Ember, an imprint of Random House Children's Books, a division of Random House, Inc., New York. Originally published in paperback in Australia by Allen & Unwin, Sydney, in 2010. Subsequently published in hardcover in the United States by Alfred A. Knopf, an imprint of Random House Children's Books, New York, in 2012.

Ember and the E colophon are registered trademarks of Random House, Inc.

Extracts on pages 143 and 227 copyright © by Kate Jennings. Reproduced by kind permission of the author.

This project has been assisted by the Australian government through the Australia Council, its arts funding and advisory body.

Visit us on the Web! randomhouse.com/teens

Educators and librarians, for a variety of teaching tools, visit us at RHTeachersLibrarians.com

The Library of Congress has cataloged the hardcover edition of this work as follows:
Buzo, Laura.
[Good oil]
Love and other perishable items / Laura Buzo. — 1st American ed.
p. cm.
Summary: A fifteen-year-old Australian girl gets her first job and first crush on her unattainable university-aged co-worker, as both search for meaning in their lives.
ISBN 978-0-375-87000-2 (trade) — ISBN 978-0-375-97000-9 (lib. bdg.) —
ISBN 978-0-375-98674-1 (ebook) — ISBN 978-0-307-92974-7 (pbk.)
[1. Love—Fiction. 2. Friendship—Fiction. 3. Maturation (Psychology)—Fiction.
4. Work—Fiction. 5. Australia—Fiction.] I. Title.
PZ7.B98319Lo 2012 [Fic]—dc23 2011037579

Printed in the United States of America

10 9 8 7 6 5 4 3 2 1

First Ember Edition 2013

To absent friends

Spheres of No Influence
January

Lights Up

"I'm writing a play," says Chris, leaning over the counter of my cash register. "It's called *Death of a Customer*. Needless to say, it's set here." He jerks his head toward the aisles lined with groceries and lit with harsh fluorescent bars.

It takes me a moment to place the reference, but then I remember *Death of a Salesman* from when Dad took me to see the play last year.

"Sounds good."

"Want to be in it?"

I nod eagerly.

"Cool. We're going to the pub after work to workshop it. You should come."

"Who—" I squeak. "Who's going?"

"Oh, Ed, Bianca, Donna . . . people."

I am only three weeks past my fifteenth birthday, but my braces came off a month ago, so I could possibly slip into a pub looks-wise. Trouble is, my scorching unease would give me away to the door guy, and even if by some miracle it didn't, I am terrified of interacting socially with my coworkers. Except Chris.

Donna is my age, but she has no trouble keeping up with them. She wears eye makeup and pulls it off. She wears calf-high black boots with purple laces. She smokes and has been kicked out of home by her father several times. She has serious street cred. Unlike me. Ed is nice enough, but he's eighteen and kind of vagued out all the time. Bianca is twenty-three and ignores me so consistently that it must be deliberate. I am not going to the pub with them.

"I can't," I say.

"Why not?"

"I have homework."

This is not a lie. I'm struggling in math as it is. Getting behind will make it worse. My shift ends at nine o'clock, so even if I go straight home, I won't get to my homework until nine-forty at least.

Chris's face contracts in annoyance. "So? I have a two-thousand-word paper due on Friday. Life must still be lived."

"I can't."

"You can do it in the morning."

I shake my head.

"I'll take you home afterward. You'll be home by midnight."

Now I'm torn. Two hours of sharing him with the others and then I'd be rewarded by fifteen minutes of having him all to myself on the walk home.

"Ed's got his parents' car tonight. We'll drop you right at your door."

Crap. "I can't."

"Fine, whatever," he says, withdrawing his presence like a parent confiscating a favorite toy. He stalks off in the direction of the deli, probably to ask "She's-big-she's-blond-she-works-in-the-deli" Georgia to go to the pub and join the collaboration on his dramatic masterpiece.

As Chris's name for her suggests, Georgia is in fact blond, has big breasts, and manages to wear the deli's white uniform in a way that is quite fetching. However, my point of envy is the fact that, at eighteen, she is a good three years closer in age to Chris.

"No fair," I mutter as he disappears from sight.

Land of Dreams

Chris never refers to the Coles supermarket we work at as "Coles." He calls it the Land of Dreams. On nights and weekends, the Land of Dreams is staffed by part-timers. Mainly high school students (me, Street Cred Donna and several others who go to public schools in the area), university students (Chris, Kathy, Kelly, Stuart) and a few other "young adult" types who obviously haven't yet decided what to "do" with their lives and are working at Coles while they figure it out (Ed, Bianca, Andy).

Come to think of it, that may be a bit of an assumption on my part. I've never actually seen Ed, Bianca or Andy grappling with the mystery of their existence or their place in the universe. They're just *there*. Ed to earn enough money to support his pot habit. Bianca to flirt with the teenage checkout boys. And Andy? Well, who knows; he rarely says anything.

I started work at the Land of Dreams last year, almost on the dot of age fourteen and nine months. This was a move motivated by a passionate aversion to asking my parents for money and the knowledge that there was not much of it going spare around our way in any case. Money is never openly discussed in my house, but I suspect that last year was a bit tough. My sister Liza moved out to go to university in Bathurst, and my dad was longer than usual between jobs. Asking for money began to stress me out. Dad would say he didn't have any cash and to ask Mum. Mum would sigh and look pissed off and give it to me with less than good grace. So I thought, *Enough of that.*

I went to the local shopping center and asked for work at every shop except the butcher (eww) and the tobacconist (evil). I really had to push myself to go in each time and not stumble over my words. I did stumble a bit, but most took my number and said they'd call if something came up. One week later a lady from Coles rang and asked me to come in for an interview after school. I started a week after that.

The morning of my first training shift I came down to breakfast. Dad was reading the newspaper and Mum was wiping up some Ovaltine spilled on the floor by my little sister.

"I've got a job at Coles," I said.

"At Metro Fair," I added.

"On the checkout," I concluded.

Mum nodded as she wiped.

"Good," said Dad, looking up from his newspaper for a second. "That's good, darling."

Ever since then I've been working three nights a week from four till nine, and from noon till four on Saturday or sometimes Sunday.

I've got my work routine down pat. At the final school bell I make my way to my locker amid hordes of girls stampeding to freedom. My locker is next to my best friend Penny's, so we always meet at the end of the day. I change out of my school uniform and into my black work pants and black shoes.

"Sweetie pie," Penny often says, watching me struggle into my work pants and hoick my tunic over my head, trying not to take my shirt up with it. "There's got to be an easier way."

She holds the shirt down for me and catches me if I lose my balance while unknotting the laces of my school shoes. I stuff my school uniform into my backpack and gather up my textbooks and folders. Then we join the throng and negotiate our way outside.

As Australia is "girt by sea," my school is "girt by road." Major six-lane traffic arteries on all sides. Heavy on the fumes. When it rains, great swaths of dirty, oily water collect in the gutters. Then buses roar past and send gallons of energetic spray up onto the pavement. In the five yards between the curb and the school fence there's no escape. It's bad enough if you get drenched while waiting for the bus home, but getting caught on the way to the school gates in the morning seriously blows.

My afternoon bus is the 760. I never get a seat, as the boys from the brother school next door are ferocious pushers. Some of my most disillusioning school moments have involved getting stuck in a crush of twenty or so teenage boys who have no qualms whatsoever about going straight over the top of anyone smaller or less inclined to push. They shove, swear, show off and certainly aren't above hair-pulling. Vindication sometimes comes with a certain bus driver who won't let any of the boys on until all the girls are aboard. The boys jeer under their breath as we girls file on, and you can bet they're even more merciless the next day.

Most days I'm happy to hang back and see if I can squeeze on at the end. But on workdays, I have to get on or I'll be late. The 760 gets me to Coles by four, whereupon I don my red scarf and name badge, shove my stuff into my locker, check the roster to see what register I'm on that shift and jump on.

The Ropes

"Miss Amelia Hayes, welcome to the Land of Dreams!"

The boy grinned at me and motioned me into the same tiny room I'd been interviewed in.

"I'll leave you to it then," said the manager, and she closed the door.

The boy and I regarded each other for a moment. I judged him to be about twenty. His features were unremarkable, but his face was open, immediately warm and engaging; he seemed to twinkle.

"I," he said, "am Chris, your friendly staff trainer. You'll be with me for three four-hour shifts. I will call you Grasshopper and you will call me Sensei, and I will share with you what I know. Right?"

"Okay." I smiled. It was hard not to.

"Now," he said, fumbling in his pants pocket. "Where's your . . . ? Got it." He pulled out a name badge that said TRAINEE. "This baby is yours for three days, and after that, if you play your cards right, you'll get your very own to love and cherish for all your days."

He approached me and fastened it to my shirt. I wasn't sure where to look.

"Just so you know, I'm open to all kinds of bribery."

"Good to know."

"Now let's get out there."

Chris taught me how to pack groceries in such a way as to incur the overall least amount of wrath from the customer. However, he stressed, you can't please everyone. He taught me about the more obscure fruits and vegetables: swedes, rambutan, jackfruit, persimmon, durian, tamarillo, dragon fruit, star fruit, okra. And the many different kinds of apples: Fuji, Braeburn, Pink Lady, Bonza, Jonathan, Sundowner, Red Delicious, Golden Delicious, Granny Smith. Then there were brushed potatoes, washed potatoes, Desiree potatoes, new potatoes, Kipfler potatoes and Red Pontiac Potatoes. At the beginning, he said, I would have to look up the different codes for each of them, which would be tedious and slow, but soon enough they would all be in my head.

Chris also told me that every so often I would have a complete jerk come through my register.

"The important thing to remember," said Chris, "is It's Not About You. Some people are just pricks. And that's not only true in here."

On the third night of training it was time for me to serve my first customers. Chris stayed beside me for the first few and then hovered close by for an hour, twinkling encouragement and appearing at my side if I was struggling with anything. At about eight o'clock the rush had finished and he sidled over.

"I think you've earned a break, Youngster." He smiled and put up the CLOSED sign on my register. "I'll buy you a Coke."

We sat drinking our Cokes in the deserted food court of the shopping center. All the shops were in darkness, with their security shutters down.

"So, Amelia, how old would you be?"

"I'm fifteen. Almost."

"Wow, you really are a youngster."

"Guess so."

"You like school?"

"Yeah. Yeah, I like it most of the time. Not math, though."

"The best thing about finishing school is not having to do math anymore. You mark my words."

"Can't wait."

"Favorite subject?"

"English. Definitely. My teacher this year is a bit weird, but still ..."

"Your love is strong and true."

I looked at him. "What?"

"For English."

"Oh yeah. For sure. I just hope I don't get her for senior English."

"Got someone else in mind?"

"Miss McFadden. Everyone wants Miss McFadden."

"But they can't all have her."

"No, they can't."

It's really easy to talk to him, I thought.

"What about you?" I asked.

"Me. I'm in my last year at University of New South Wales."

"What do you take?"

"Major in English with a minor in sociology. I'm thinking of staying on another year to make it a double major."

"Then what?"

"Oh, don't you start," he said sharply.

Chastened, I drank my Coke.

"Got brothers or sisters?" he asked.

"Older sister, Liza. She's away at uni. Charles Sturt. Lives in Bathurst in some share house."

"Half her luck." He grimaced. "I'm with the folks."

"You don't get along?"

"They're nice people. It's not bad. It's just ... It's gone on too long. But there's no other choice. So ..." He trailed off.

"And my other sister has just turned three."

"Three! Wow."

"I know."

"Contraception doesn't work in the top drawer."

"My parents know that now."

We laughed.

"She's super-gorgeous, though," I said, my heart swelling a little at the thought of Jessica's soft chubby cheeks and philosophical musings. That morning she had approached me while I ate my toast. *Amelia.* She laid one of her hands gently over mine. *My hands don't come off. They're attached to my body.* So true.

"Got a boyfriend?"

"What? No. How would that even happen?"

I hadn't really talked to a boy since primary school. My only male contact was with the pushers and shovers on the bus, and they fell short of every expectation. *Talking to them wouldn't be like this,* I thought.

"Got a girlfriend?" I countered.

He twisted the pull tab on his Coke can and then pulled it off. "No." He threw the can in the direction of a trash can a few yards away. It missed, clanged against the metal and hit the ground.

"We'd better get back in there."

I nodded and pushed back my chair.

"Oh, and you should join the union, Youngster. It doesn't cost much and by God you'll get screwed around here."

The weeks went on and I settled into the routine of going to work after school. It was a little harder to keep up with schoolwork, but nothing that couldn't be remedied by late-night caffeine hits and working through the odd lunch period. Chris often brought drafts of his uni essays into work for me to read during my breaks. His favorite course was the History of Popular Culture. His essays were littered with references to his favorite films, which I soon learned were along the lines of *Alien*, *Rambo*, *Platoon*, *Apocalypse Now* and *The Godfather*. So different from what we were studying at school. He asked me what I thought of his work and he listened to my replies.

"So, Youngster," he said one day, fixing me with an eagle eye. "Why did Barnes shoot Elias?"

"Why did— Who?"

"Barnes! He shot Elias. Why?"

"I don't know what you're—"

"Don't—do not tell me you haven't seen *Platoon*."

I obliged and remained silent.

"What do they teach you at that school?"

Another day, in line to pick up our pay slips at the back office: "So the mother ship in *Alien* clearly draws on feminist theory, don'tcha think?"

"I don't watch horror movies." I mean it. Not ever. They make me scared. Scared of being alone in the house. Scared of being alone upstairs at night. Scared of walking home from work in the dark. Penny can watch scary movies and be completely unaffected. She can watch *The Silence of the Lambs* in bed and then fall sweetly asleep. I didn't sleep for a week after we watched it last year. Never again.

"It's not horror, Youngster; it's science fiction. Trailblazing science fiction."

Each conversation with Chris seemed to prompt an exhausting mix of excitement and forehead-slapping embarrassment at my inability to keep up with the references and in-jokes. Real or perceived. I go to an all-girls school where people are bent on studying. I wasn't used to talking to boys at all, let alone grown-up ones with university essays to write and incredible charisma. So, so far out of my depth.

Christmas

I worked Christmas Eve, as did Chris and most of the other part-timers. He finished his shift an hour before me and spent a good half hour doing his man-about-the-supermarket routine: entertaining the girls; engaging in serious-looking talks with the managers, his arms crossed, nodding with a furrowed brow; counseling Ed at the service desk about his life choices, or lack thereof. It was amazing how he was able to talk to anyone and everyone with confidence. I wasn't the only one who reveled in the easiness of talking to Chris. Everyone had a better shift when Chris was on.

After the routine had concluded, he disappeared into one of the aisles for a couple of minutes and reappeared carrying a bunch of flowers. He walked past the checkouts on his way to the exit.

I was focused on the task of maneuvering a huge frozen turkey into a plastic bag, but I was acutely aware of his movements. (It was a skill I'd developed. At any given time, in addition to performing my checkout duties, I could tell you where Chris was, where he had been and when he was due to finish.) It looked as though he was going to walk out without saying goodbye or merry Christmas or anything.

At the last moment he paused at my checkout, threw the flowers down on the counter and muttered, "Those are for you, Youngster. Merry Christmas." And barreled on out.

I looked from the flowers to the exit and back again.

I wiped the icy turkey residue from my hands onto my pants and moved the flowers underneath the register. They had a Coles staff-purchases seal on them and a sticker that said REDUCED FOR QUICK SALE.

After work I walked home hugging my flowers with a queer fluttery excitement in my chest.

"Who are those from?" asked my mother, in front of a gaggle of Christmas Eve relatives, as I walked in the front door.

"Um . . . someone from work," I managed.

She raised one eyebrow. "Well. We'd better put them in a vase."

I was distraught when they died a few days later and Mum insisted they be thrown out.

All December, I'd looked ridiculously forward to shifts when Chris would be working, especially if he was on a checkout within earshot of me, or better still in front of me, so I could watch him chatting to his customers, doing that thing he did. He could have a conversation with absolutely anyone.

He was not to be messed with, though, for all his chumminess with the managers. The store's air-conditioning busted a few days before Christmas, and several of us checkout staff almost fainted from the heat, thanks to the heavy felt Santa hats we were required to wear. Maybe those hats would make sense at the North Pole, but here in Australia, Christmas falls in the dead of summer. Most of us cursed and bitched as we wiped away the sweat that ran down into our eyes, but we continued to scan and pack groceries. Not Chris. He petitioned management to have the Santa hats abandoned until the air-conditioning was fixed. Management remained unmoved and said the Santa hats were an important part of creating a Christmassy atmosphere. Chris went to the union. Pretty soon the Santa hats were a thing of the past.

Chris, the hero of the hour, personally removed the Santa hat from my overheated head, waved it triumphantly in the air and threw it under the counter. He winked at me, leaned in and whispered in my ear with playful conspiracy, "Rage against the machine, Youngster."

And, almost imperceptibly, his hand touched my arm before he returned to his own register. It was the first time that any of his skin had touched any of mine.

Working alongside Chris transformed five hours of boredom into a wonderland of banter and laughter. I surreptitiously scanned the roster to see which shifts we were scheduled on together and always made sure my hair was washed and as anti-frizzed as possible on those days. When school holidays began, we worked a lot of the same shifts. That fluttery feeling in my chest felt as though it was starting to bruise my rib cage.

The final nail in the coffin of my sanity came one night toward the close of business. Chris was lounging over my register, chatting. I think we were talking about social hierarchies in high school as compared to social hierarchies at university.

"I'm not saying that Beautiful People don't have the right to exist," I remember saying. "I'm not saying that they should be rounded up and taken to an island. I'm just saying that they are never, ever to be trusted because they can never know what it's like not to be Beautiful and their priority will always be being Beautiful with other Beautiful People."

"So you think that everyone should know their place and be happy in it, and not seek to have any congress beyond that?"

Bianca (who was the service supervisor, and so the boss of us) barked at Chris from down at the service desk, where she was delicately adjusting the uniform red bow tie of one of the better-looking checkout boys. "Chris! Back to work!"

He didn't move right away. He looked at me and, with full eye contact for maximum impact, said, "You are the real thing, Youngster. I hope you will never change," before moving slowly back to his own register.

I know a compliment when I hear one, even if I don't fully understand the nature of it. The hammer shot that last nail in with one strong blow.

One afternoon in January, I sit on the couch watching TV with my little sister. Jess likes to watch TV snuggled up to me. All right, all right—I like watching TV snuggled up to her. We are watching *Sesame Street*. Apart from wondering whatever happened to Grundgetta, I'm not really paying attention. I'm mulling over the last few weeks at work, in particular thinking about Chris, when it comes to me. The whir and fog in my mind suddenly clear and leave three words standing tall and indisputable:

I love Chris.

My tummy feels weird. I sit there pondering for what must be a long time, letting Jess watch the older kids' programs that are on later and later. Eventually my father comes in and starts making a whisky and soda for himself and my mother. Whisky and soda signals six o'clock and time for me to get up and set the table for dinner. In love or no.

The Kathy Virus
and Other Anomalies

"Fishing off the company pier," as I have overheard Chris refer to it, is a common practice among the part-time staff at Coles. Bianca, for example, is twenty-three and has been going out with Andy from Canned Goods, age eighteen, for some months. This is in addition to the bow-tie adjusting she indulges in on a regular basis with most of the other male staff members. Like I said earlier, Andy is a pretty quiet guy. I imagine he just does what he is told. They must both get something out of the relationship—I just have no idea what it is.

"Sex," says Chris when I ask him. "They both get sex."

Lots of the younger girls have crushes on Ed, who, even I have to admit, is pretty good-looking. He is also aloof, adding to his appeal. Sadly for the girls, he is generally too stoned to take advantage of their attentions. Chris can frequently be seen leaning over the counter of the service desk berating him. "You have to be in it to win it, Edward!" and the like.

The yawning six-year chasm between my age and Chris's is not the only fly in the proverbial ointment of this "loving Chris" business. I'm not even sure what "getting" Chris would involve; all I know is I want him. I want to be enfolded by him somehow, and to possess him. To have unfettered and exclusive access to him all the time. To feel how I feel around him all the time. To know that he loves being around me too. To feel more of his skin on my skin.

But Chris seems to be in perpetual pursuit of another girl from work called Kathy Rushworth. She's twenty-two and studying primary education at the same university as Chris. Like Bianca, she is a supervisor and so is sort of Chris's boss. He refers to his long-standing crush as the Kathy virus, as it seems to take a relapsing-remitting course.

"Got a raging case of it today, Youngster," he mutters, pushing a cart past my register with white knuckles, watching Kathy talking animatedly to Stuart Green from Canned Goods at the service desk.

The following week Chris declares, "It's in remission!" and declines Kathy's invitation to go to the pub after work. Instead, he hangs around after his shift advising me on my English assignment.

Kathy is dark, pretty, small—elfin even—and completely uninterested in Chris. Except, strangely, when the Kathy virus is in remission. Then she bombards him with a campaign of arm-touching (signature move), bow-tie adjusting (borrowed from Bianca) and leaning over his register giving him her undivided, head-cocked-to-one-side attention. An immediate relapse of the Kathy virus invariably follows.

That Kathy needs a can of reduced-for-quick-sale Spam pegged at the back of her head, and I reckon I'm the woman for the job. They're stacked within easy reach of my register.

After glaring at the Chris-and-Kathy spectacle for the whole shift from my dress-circle vantage point at register seven, I walk home through the deserted mall and dark streets.

Fifteen-year-old checkout girls are in no position to compete with someone like Kathy. Even Street Cred Donna would be struggling to make serious inroads with Chris. (Which, by the way, I am totally convinced she is. I am not the only youngster looking up to Chris with a thumping heart. She just shows it differently. I can spot a rival at twenty paces.) She has recently added a tattoo of barbed wire encircling her upper right arm (as a sixteenth-birthday present to herself) and has her mother's name tattooed on her other arm. You can't see her tats—her work shirt covers them. Chris told me about them.

My sixteenth birthday is months and months away. I have no tats. I don't smoke. I have no idea how to wear makeup, and now that my older sister has moved away to live on campus, I have no one to teach me. I don't stand a chance. I know this.

I turn my key in the front door and grunt a greeting to my mother, who is folding laundry in front of the TV. Dad is away this week.

I sling my heavy backpack to the floor next to the couch, sit down beside Mum and take my shoes off.

"How was your day?" I ask her.

She doesn't answer. Never a good sign.

"What's the matter?"

"Nothing."

I wait uneasily. "Bad day at work?"

"No."

"Jess throwing tantrums?"

"No."

Her movements folding the clothes are jerky and angry, and she slams every folded item down on its pile. Her face is tired, her mouth a straight line.

"What's wrong?" I ask again.

"Nothing!"

I won't get it out of her. I'm short on time anyway. Got hours of homework and it's almost nine-thirty.

"Is there any dinner?"

"In the oven."

I eat standing up in the kitchen, rinse my plate, collect my backpack and climb the stairs. When I reach the top, it is dark, except for the green glow of Jess's night-light in the end bedroom. English first, I think as I snap on my bedroom light.

My English teacher, Mrs. Cumming, who I have for the second year running, has a very "interpretive" approach to the tenth-grade syllabus. She's decided that the first text this year is Sylvia Plath's The Bell Jar. I'm halfway through it. The main character has tried to kill herself a couple of times now. She's also really uncomfortable with the fact that she's a virgin. She looks around and divides people into two categories—people who have had sex and people who have not. That's something I can relate to a bit. No one in my immediate peer group has crossed that Rubicon (I don't think!), but still, I live in the world. And I'm in love with a twenty-one-year-old. So it crosses my mind. Whenever anything to do with sex comes up in conversation with Chris, he gives me this sympathetic look, like he doesn't want to scare me, or confront me. Like I'm too delicate. Scare me! I want to shout. Confront me! I'm not so breakable—go on, try!

I am nowhere near sold on The Bell Jar but keep plowing through it because Chris nodded his approval the week before.

He came into the staff room on my break and saw me reading it. "Sylvia Plath, eh? Hard-core."

"Yes. Yes, it is hard-core."

"This is the weird English teacher, right?"

"Yes. Yes, she is weird."

"Want a coffee?" He got a stack of Styrofoam cups out of the cupboard and prized the lid off the massive tin of International Roast so generously provided. Yuck.

"Yes. Thank you."

I closed the book and waited for him to sit down. A cup of International Roast with Chris at 8:15 p.m. on a school night. Plastic chairs in a windowless room. It was the high point of my day. It was the high point of my life.

The margins of all my exercise books are filled with letter Cs in various colors, fonts and incarnations. I stare out of classroom windows, wondering what he is doing. I imagine him at university, taking lecture notes, hanging out with his friends at the uni bar, putting in his two cents' worth at the sociology seminar he loves. And, of course, talking to girls. Grown-up girls at university. Girls who can go drinking with him after class. Girls his own age who he could confidently introduce to his family and friends. Girls who know how to dress and wear makeup. Girls who have had sex. Girls who study the same texts as him. Girls who stand a chance in hell.

I'm quieter than usual during the lunch period. I lie on my back on the grass, my head resting on my backpack, surrounded by the voices of my friends, and look up at the bright blue sky. Penny sits next to my inert form, talking to Ally and Eleni, but occasionally she waves a hand in front of my face and shakes her head, laughing.

"She all right?" someone asks.

"Sure," says Penny. "She's just in her happy place." Penny drops her hand onto mine and briefly squeezes it.

The six lanes of traffic on the other side of the fence hum to my right. I close my eyes and imagine Chris brushing my hair away from my neck with warm hands. I open my eyes again. My lips feel like they are burning.

At work, I hear that Street Cred Donna's dad has belted her

and kicked her out of the house. Egged on in large part by the stepmother. Her real mother remarried and moved to America when Donna was twelve. Up ahead of me on register twelve Donna is serving customers, her eyes puffy and her shirt unironed.

During my break, I walk out to the back dock, eating my granola bar, and happen upon Chris and Donna. She's crying. Her face is streaked with eye makeup, her shoulders are shaking and she smokes with nicotine-stained fingers. Chris is gently stroking her back. Catching sight of me over the top of her bowed head, he wordlessly waves me away.

I wonder, despicably, *If I invent a similar crisis, will he stroke my back too?*

Daylight

The next day I sit in math with Penny in our usual spot—far left, second row from the front. I knit my brows together and attempt to adjust to the hard, cold daylight. To the way things are. It's *never going to happen.*

"Probably not," says Penny, reading my mind and telling it like it is in her usual style.

I sigh and look out at the park on the other side of the road. I can see a PE class of unfortunates jogging up a hellish incline. *Unless,* I think, *my momentary flirtation with reality dissolving, I can somehow infiltrate the older set at work. Get him to associate me with his contemporaries. Maybe I could get hold of his reading list for uni. Maybe I could start smoking, get a fake ID and start going to the pub. Maybe I could learn to stomach beer and how to order it. Maybe I could buy some clothes aside from jeans and T-shirts. Maybe I could learn some new and super-impressive words. Convince him that I am a twenty-year-old trapped in the body of a minor.*

"I could do it," I say to Penny. "It could be done. Right?"

"Oh, sweetie. I think it would be hard to pull off. And anyway, he probably likes that you are different from his usual world."

She's right; it would be hard to pull off. Observe this monumental fuckup from last week.

Against all the odds, Chris had run out after me into the street after I had knocked off from a Sunday shift. "Oi! Youngster!"

I'd turned to face him and instinctively stood up straighter at his nearness.

"Look, some of us are going back to Ed's for a bowl. Do you want to come?"

"A bowl? A bowl of what?"

He rolls his eyes. "Um, I don't know. . . . A bowl of ice cream. What do you think?"

Ice cream? I'm on a dairy-free diet because I'm lactose intolerant. And Ed lives several suburbs away; how would I get home afterward? Would Mum and Dad notice that I was late and want answers? Mrs. Hulme wanted chapters two and three of The Great War summarized by the next day. But this was the chance of a lifetime!

I agonized. I shifted my weight from one foot to the other and finally stammered, "I—I can't." (Eloquence is just one of my gifts.) "Too much homework . . . and . . . and I can't really have ice cream. Just . . . just soy ice cream . . . since it's non-dairy . . ." My voice trailed off.

"Um, don't worry about it," he said, edging away.

Bugger!

I could see Ed, Bianca, Andy, Kathy (damn her!) and Donna (heartsick) assembling at the staff exit, waiting for Chris. Bloody Donna has managed to get hip to their jive. Look at her, fumbling in her canvas satchel for a cigarette, lighting it, then Bianca's, with her Zippo. The metallic clicking sound that it made when she flicked the lid back down against her palm seemed to encapsulate everything I was lacking. Then she took a drag and blew a steady plume of smoke, looking out from behind it with equally smoky eyes. (I had found some kohl in my mother's makeup bag the week before and tried to re-create Donna's look on my own eyes. It just looked stupid.)

"I shouldn't have asked you anyway," he was saying. "You go home and do your homework."

I don't want to go home and do my homework! I want to come with you! I want to be out late at Ed's house and fall asleep on his couch with my head in your lap. I'll eat ice cream! I'll do whatever it takes!

"All right. See you."

"See you."

I must have looked crestfallen.

"Are you still studying World War I?" he asked, taking pity on me like the big baby I was.

"Yeah," I replied in a small voice.

"You should read *All Quiet on the Western Front*. I'll bring it in for you on Tuesday night, okay?"

"Okay."

He turned on his heel and went back to join the others.

I'd walked home muttering curses and clenching my fists. When I arrived, the house was dark and quiet. I rummaged around for the phone number for Liza's share house, took the phone into my room and dialed in the number.

It rang and rang before the beep and a female voice inquired somewhat uncertainly, "Hello?" over very loud music. I asked several times to speak to my sister before the female voice undertook to go off and find her for me. About five minutes later I heard fumbling and then finally Liza's voice.

"Hello?"

"Lizey. It's me."

"He-ey, little sis! How're you?"

"Yeah, fine. Look, I was wondering, um, what's a bowl?"

Mystified silence.

"You know, like, if people are 'having a bowl' . . . What's a bowl?"

"Oh. It's a kind of pipe thingy you use . . . you know, like a bong."

"Ooooh, right."

"Got it?"

"Yep. Thanks. Better go. Lots of homework. Bye."

I hung up and sat motionless on my bed. Then I dialed the number again.

"Lizey? Me again. What . . . what's a bong?"

"It's a water pipe for smoking pot in."

"Oh."

"Why are you asking?"

"Um . . ."

"Are you getting on it?"

"No, no . . . I'm not 'getting on it.'" So, so not, I thought. Almost, but totally blew it.

"Well," mused Liza, "if you're going to try it, you should come up one weekend and I'll get some for you. That way I can keep an eye on you. And give you the talk."

"Thanks. Maybe I will."

"You'll love the talk."

"I'm sure I will. I miss you."

"Yeah . . . I miss you too."

Liar. She was having an absolute ball up there, I could tell. I lay back on my bed. The indignity! Why did my parents have to have me fifteen years ago? Why couldn't they have had me eighteen years ago? Then at least I'd have had a fighting chance of knowing what a bowl was, and that would be a fine thing!

A Valid Lifestyle Choice

For those who are unfamiliar with the lifestyle, you do get used to having a whopping, pointless crush. By using the word *lifestyle*, I don't mean to imply that it is in any way glamorous or desirable. Just that it becomes a normal part of everyday life, and your body gets kind of attuned to functioning on that plane. Your friends and teachers get used to you staring out of windows when you used to be quite sharp. You stare out of all kinds of windows: classroom windows, bus windows, your bedroom window, over the sink and out of the kitchen window. Your central nervous system speeds up when the object of your affection is near, or expected to be near. Your senses sharpen, particularly peripheral vision. I am acutely aware of Chris's movements at work. I see him approaching even when I'm studying a bag of beans to distinguish whether they're pinto beans or lima. I know which girls he's talked to throughout the shift. I know when he's preoccupied or playful by the way he moves. I know when he's pissed off that Kathy has been talking to Stuart Green from Canned Goods. I know it all. Sometimes I mutter his name under my breath like a madwoman.

I'm grateful for the twenty-minute walk home after work as it gives me time to unclench my muscles and recover from the strain of watching Chris flirt with the endless parade of my competition.

Aside from the constant threat of the Kathy virus (don't know why I say *threat*, as if I'm actually in the running) and the effortless superiority of Street Cred Donna and Georgia from the deli, there are quite a few new female part-timers. One of them is a sixteen-year-old called Sveta Tarasova. Her name alone conjures up images of gorgeous Russian Bond girls who could kill you with their thighs after you have succumbed to their charms. Villainesses who wear slinky black dresses, have long dark hair, smoke cigarettes from a cigarette holder, drink vodka martinis and bat their smoky eyes, saying, "Da, darlink." Later on in the penthouse, *afterward*, if you came around to their way of thinking, they would mix you another vodka martini, bring it over to you and toast, "To crime, darlink." *Oh God, maybe she's going to kill Chris with her thighs.*

Or maybe I'm getting a bit carried away. Let's face it; it wouldn't be the first time. Unfortunately, Sveta actually is extremely slim, with long dark straight hair. She doesn't say much. She has killer legs, and at work she wears a very short black skirt with black tights and Mary Jane–style shoes. After watching her reach up high to put some home-delivery bags on top of the trolley, Chris and I find out that she wears stockings. Real stockings. The kind that are held up by garters. We are treated to a generous glimpse of them while she strains with the heavy bags.

"Oh ... my ... God," murmurs Chris.

I'm incensed. Who does that? Who wears stockings with garters? There are plenty of normal stockings to be had. Why can't she buy a pair of 'em like everyone else?

Chris is gone in seconds, down to the service desk to tell Ed about this unexpected and heaven-sent eyeful.

To add insult to injury, Sveta also wears a demure little black cardigan over her white work shirt, probably a deliberately titillating juxtaposition for the garters. Bitch.

I overhear Chris asking her to have a coffee with him after work. Of course. Why wouldn't he? Nothing I can do about it.

There is actually nothing I can do about most things, I realize walking home. Being a slightly frumpy fifteen-year-old does not lend itself to much agency in any field. Chris is writing an essay on E. P. Thompson and has been telling me all about "structure versus agency" at various intervals.

I live at home with my parents. I have to do as I am told there.

I go to work. I have to do as I am told there.

I go to school. I have to do as I am told there too.

I never get a seat on the school bus because the pushers and shovers defeat me. As soon as I turned fourteen, I put on a few pounds, and no matter how I crash-diet and run around the park, I can't seem to shed them. My sister Liza lives in a big share house with other students and tells tales of parties and boyfriends every time we speak on the phone. I live in a small room in my parents' house. My hair frizzes up around my face no matter how much I comb it down. Chris keeps on flirting with the other girls at work no matter how much I will him to stop. There's not a single thing I can do about any of it.

One day last week I'd been mouthing off to Chris about *Othello*, which we had just started studying at school. He'd listened to me with his head slightly cocked to one side, offering small arguments that I talked over.

"Why is it called *The Tragedy of Othello*—should be *The Tragedy of Desdemona!*"

"Well, it's a tragedy for her too, but you know he's the main protag—"

"He kills his wife! Just kills her! I mean, what kind of psycho kills his wife and then gets to be the hero of the play?"

"He's a tragic hero, Youngster. He has a fatal flaw—they all do."

"It's not his tragedy! It's Desdemona's!"

"But the play is not *about* her, Youngs—"

"How small a man is he? He's this big war hero, but he's so insecure that he believes all that crap about his wife. Who loves him, the poor woman. Big mistake. But how was she to know?"

"He was willfully deceived by Iago. If someone is that good at deception, it's easy to believe them."

"It shouldn't have been that easy. Men!"

Chris gave up.

"You should get your own TV show, Youngster," he'd said.

Blimey, I thought, picturing his face yet again. I should have my own TV show, all right. It would be called *Lifestyles of the Young and Powerless. Lifestyles of Them That Had a Mouthful of Metal Until a Short Time Ago. Lifestyles of Them That Still Let Their Mums Choose Their Clothes and Spent Last Saturday Night at Their Best Mate's House Studying.* I'm a disgrace. The only high points in my life are those rare moments when Chris offers to walk me home after work and listens to my rants with what appears to be tender amusement. I have become a bit of a ranter, I must admit. School, work, the disrespect with which my dad addressed my mum the other morning, the injustice of the universe, the crappy marks I keep getting in math, *Madame Bovary*, how one of my teachers drops the s in *hubris* like you pronounce *debris*.

"Breathe, Youngster, breathe. You're an Angry Young Woman."

But he listens.

The Purple Notebook

August 5

Time: 2 p.m.

Location: Uni library

Hours rostered at Coles this week: 22

Uni essays to research and write: 3 (and a presentation)

Health: head hurts, shoulders hurt

Cars owned by myself, Christopher John Harvey: nil

Hours spent waiting at bus stops this week: 4.2

Status report on the Search for the Perfect Woman: fruitless but ongoing

Money saved from Coles job this year: $250

Money spent on random shit including alcohol, caffeine, aspirin, angsty music and one or two items of Young People's Clothing: the rest of it

Mum and Dad were asking this morning if I'm going to have a twenty-first. Hmm. This would probably involve assembling the usual suspects and having a party in the backyard. I'll undoubtedly get tanked, as will everyone else, and it might be rather a pity for the parentals to have to see me in such a state. So I'd just as soon do all that at the pub and have a night I will try to remember rather than one I wish I could forget. . . .

The uni bar, bless it, has a special on Long Island iced teas this week. I have to work after class this afternoon, but tomorrow afternoon I'm fucking going. I'll be there as soon as they roll up the metal shutters, demanding my value-for-money oblivion in a tall glass. I have my History of American Foreign Policy double lecture in the afternoon and I'm sure as hell not going to it sober.

Now, dear reader (of whom there are none, but I can't seem

to stop writing that), it is 2:45 p.m. and time for me to leave for my history tute. If I leave right now, and take a circuitous route via the physics building, I may run into Kathy. For the benefit of the new notebook, Kathy is at present—once again—the focus of my Search for the Perfect Woman. She seems to look hotter every day, and while she pretty much ignores me at uni, I do seem to be able to engage her at odd moments when we are at work. She's dropped down to two shifts per week, though, so that's a bit crappy. The upshot is that I pretty much don't have a chance with her. And, you know, thank God, because if I did, I'd have to give up my lifestyle of soul-wrenching loneliness and sexual frustration. I'm too good at it to quit now. I could brood for Australia.

Harvey out.

P.S. I didn't think about Michaela for a good several-hour stretch today. Go figure.

August 14

I'm writing outside on the lawn today as the sun is out and blessedly warming the back of my neck. Looking forward to the summer break. I have decided to stay on to complete a second major next year after all, because the idea of leaving uni in three months' time and looking for a real job is quite frankly a little too much for me to contemplate in my (perpetually) delicate state. Seemingly as per, woke up hungover this morning, fully clothed and feeling as if something had died in my mouth. Stumbled into the shower, too ratshit even to jerk off. Put empty wine bottle into my backpack (it upsets my mother to see empty bottles on my bedside table) and left for uni. After a couple of ibuprofen and two coffees I am almost a human being again.

Coles is pissing me off royally. Now even Kathy has been made a service supervisor and no longer has to work on those godforsaken registers. I've been there as long as her! Bianca only beat me by a few weeks and she's been a supervisor for months now. They think that giving me the staff trainer role is going to placate me. Well, it's not. It's a gristly old bone and frankly they are going to have to throw me a better one. Yes, I get to torture, ridicule, perv on and flirt with (as appropriate) the unending stream of hapless teenagers that keep getting hired, but I still spend most of my time on the registers. Fuck that. If they don't make me a supervisor by the new year, I'll either quit or ask Mr. Albertella for a transfer to Perishables or something. As long as it's not to Canned Goods with that fucker Stuart Green. Anyway, I digress.

Uuuuum. Yeah. Stuff. Kathy wore a skirt and tights to work last night instead of her usual pants. So that was exciting. I was excited. I'm still excited. So excited I may have to go to Ed's for a joint or three after work tonight. Take the edge off.

It's time for an update on the Search for the Perfect Woman. The Field is as follows:

—**Kathy** Never in a million years.

—**She's-big-she's-blond-she-works-in-the-deli Georgia Sanders** Ed and Lincoln reckon it'd be a done deal if I got off my arse and did something. They're probably right—and a man is not a camel. However, I have never, ever been interested in anything she has said.

—**Lauren from sociology seminar** Pretty token, though. I hardly know her. Funky necklaces. Hates Durkheim.

—**Michaela** Never in a trillion years. Unbelievably unhealthy for me to have even written it down.

August 22

Okay. Let me begin by saying I am pretty fucking drunk, and as the wine I quaffed just now cannot possibly have hit my bloodstream yet, I will get drunker still. The reason for my drunkenness is I got a phone call from Michaela today. I was flummoxed, to say the least, at her calling. I thought I made myself perfectly clear about this sort of thing at the airport. That grisly day. But no, she calls me from Perth and starts making pleasant conversation.

She asks me how I am. She asks me how uni is going; how Mum and Dad are!?!

I ask her where she is calling from.

She hesitates—then says she is calling from Brad's place.

"Oh, how is Brad?" I ask with considerable Tone.

She balks, then recovers and says he is fine.

"Well, that's great, Michaela," I say. "I can't tell you how happy I am to hear that. Now why the fuck are you calling me?"

She says she is still hoping we can be friends.

Friends. Let me share with you, dear reader, or indeed anyone who will listen, why Michaela's hope that we "can be friends" is a vain one.

When I think about her life in Perth, I feel jealousy like a sickness. I can taste it in my mouth and feel it pulsing through every cell in my body. It expands my capillaries. It thuds in my ears. I don't mean just jealous of Brad. That's not casting the net nearly wide enough. I am jealous of her family: her parents, sisters, uncles, aunts and cousins, who see her all the time, who get to celebrate with her every Christmas and birthday. I am jealous of all her mates, who get to go for walks on the beach with her after class, who play soccer with her on Sundays, who drink with her at the session afterward, who come over to watch campy movies every Monday night. I'm jealous of the bus drivers whom she buys tickets off, for their moment of proximity when she dips her bus ticket into the ticket reader. I'm jealous of the salesclerks who get to sell her packs of chewing gum and newspapers, for the momentary greetings and brushes of skin when she hands over her money. I'm jealous of the hot water from the shower that slides over her skin and soaks into her hair. I'm jealous of the mirrors that reflect the brilliant brown warmth of her eyes. I'm jealous of the pillow on which she lays her cheek at night. Bastards, all of them. They have so much and I have nothing.

Did I mention that I have Tom Waits playing as I write? I do. It's certainly not hosing down the fire. And I'm not going to be wrapping this up anytime soon, let me tell you.

Her shoulders. That collarbone.

Brad gets to kiss her shoulders at will. He can have an all-you-can-kiss buffet of shoulders anytime he likes, and I can't bear to think about it. But suddenly I can't think of anything else.

That's why I can't be friends with her—as she dared to suggest at the airport, and by letter, and now by phone. The gall of her! *I really miss you, Chris. We were always such great mates, Chris. Let's at least salvage one part of what we had, Chris.* She's just trying to salve her own conscience.

How does she think it would work, this friendship gig? So, Michaela, my friend, my buddy, tell me, how did Brad fuck you last night? Mmmm-hmmm, mmm-hm. Yes, and tell me more, old pal—tell me from the very beginning. 'Cause you know, mate, I just can't stop visualizing a variety of scenarios. Were you sitting on the couch together watching TV after all the other roommates had straggled off to bed? Maybe you were curled up together on the couch and the program you were watching finished. As the credits rolled, he turned your beautiful face to his and kissed your soft, perfect lips. Maybe then he raised the remote up over your shoulder and turned off the TV. You climbed the stairs to his room with your arms about one another. Did he undress you on the bed, lying down, helping you struggle out of item by item of clothing, a painstaking but delicious process? Or maybe it was too cold for that and you both just quickly took your own clothes off standing up and then dived under the covers. No, come on, Michaela, you can tell me, we're all friends here! Give me the details, go on! Think of me as one of the girls. What have I been up to? Um, let's see now, bit of this, bit of that. Going to uni, going to work, jerking arhythmically like a fish on a jetty, suffocating in the vacuum left by your departure, having half-waking dreams about the time we made love for three days, hallucinating that your lips just touched my neck . . . The usual.

So messy. Holding the pen is not as easy as it was. And I'm crying.

Michaela. It costs me a lot of what I used to consider my manhood to say this, but your pleasure was more of a pleasure to me than mine. Shit, if someone had taken me aside a year ago and told me that sex could be more than the relentless search for somewhere to get off, I'd have laughed them out of whatever seedy twenty-four-hour bar they'd found me in. And then you come along with your perfect skin, your freckled shoulders, your glorious laugh, and you lay my entire life to waste. Ignorance suited me fine.

You spoke like me.

You got my jokes.

You got *me*.

You fucked me senseless.

Then you left.

The shadows on your face are flickering in the light of that candle we bought in Leura.

I see them every day.

So don't ring me up from your boyfriend's house on the other side of the continent, bursting with contentment from your great life over there, and ask me to be friends. You've made your decision; that's the end of it. I will never, ever want your friendship. I want only to possess you completely. Like it was for those three days at Leura. Nothing went bump in those nights. Nothing.

My hand hurts.

I pass out now.

Michaela.

Where are you?

I know where you are.

Fuck.

August 23

Jeez, take it easy, tiger. Don't hold back or anything, Chris. We wouldn't want you to keep the pain bottled up inside. You emotional incontinent.

Please accept my apologies for that disgraceful performance. So many f-words. What will my grandchildren think?

Probably that their grandpa had his heart ripped out, bloody and still beating, from behind his shattered rib cage by a wily Western Australian. Which is pretty much what happened.

Last night was just a temporary setback, a stumble, a blip in the getting-over-it process. I really was doing a bit better. I was dealing with the pain. Or at least successfully medicating it with ever-increasing amounts of alcohol and caffeine. When I read back over what I'd written, I seriously thought about ripping out all the pages. It was a pretty poor showing all the way through, but when I got to the bit where I was writing out the lyrics from the Dire Straits "Romeo and Juliet" song, I had to rip that out.

But then, I really want to be more honest in this diary than I have been in past ones, so everything else stays in. It's bad enough that I present such a heavily edited version of myself to my friends and family; if I start editing my diary, it will reinforce my already overwhelming tendency to be gutless. But let us *never* speak of it.

For the record, she really did cry when we made love and said she loved me like the stars above and would love me until she died. But, you know, people say shit in the moment.

All in all, there have been better days for one Christopher John Harvey.

September 2

I'm on the bus on the way to work. It is 7:05 a.m. It is also Saturday. It's just wrong, I tell you. So tired. So profoundly underwhelmed. Five more hours of my life spent at Coles, pretending to be friendly to customers, making halfhearted attempts to flirt with Kathy, being rebuffed in said attempts and rescuing fifteen-year-old checkout staff who have jammed their registers. My sister, Zoe, came into my room the other night after I got home a bit worse for wear. It was not long after the disastrous phone call from Michaela. She leaned on the doorframe and did her raising one eyebrow thing. Then she said, "You're pretty passionate about your unhappiness, aren't you, Chris?"

I looked right back at her and said, "If it's worth doing, it's worth doing well."

She just stared back, treating me to a full-strength dose of her nostril-flaring superiority. I suggested that she close the door on her way out. She banged it.

I'd better wrap up. Coles is shimmering and beckoning at the end of this block. Who can resist its siren call? It is the Land of Dreams.

September 7

I am officially struck down with the Kathy virus again. Just when you thought it was safe to go back into the staff room on your break... She's cute; she's smart; she's wearing a fitted shirt; she plays pool pretty well for a girl... It's *Kathy Virus Part IV: The Revenge.*

I would normally be cursing my stupidity for succumbing to yet another exercise in futility. In this case, though, if I could somehow manage to convert my Michaela angst into Kathy angst, it would be much easier to bear. Wanting Kathy but not having her is a lifestyle I could adjust to. It's not like I hunger to inhale the amazing smell of the skin on Kathy's neck and clavicle, because I have never experienced it in the first place. Hell, I don't even know whether she has one.

In contrast, wanting Michaela and not having her, having

inhabited a private universe with her, as the song goes, is untenable. So there. And this evening Kathy laughed at something particularly witty that I said and touched my arm. Phwoar. I need a beer. If anyone wants me, I'll be in the bar, plotting my next Kathy-related maneuver, twirling my imaginary mustache. And studiously avoiding study.

September 22

So much uni work looming. You can only hide from it up to a certain point—beyond which you are well and truly screwed. I was at that point at about this time in first year and vowed I would never return.

Dad was rather peeved at me, as I recall. He seemed to take it personally. I don't know why. I'm the one that will have to pay off the student loan debt for the subjects I failed. I suggested at the beginning of this year that perhaps he and Mum might like to pay my tuition for me up front like they did for Zoe so we get the discount. I can't remember the exact wording of Dad's response, but it was something to the effect of perhaps I'd like to go fuck myself instead.

Yeah, well, you know. Guess I'll be paying it off myself then. Assuming that I ever get a real job, that is. Maybe what Dad was really pissed off about was that he has a pansy of a son who is studying for a liberal arts degree instead of business or engineering.

Must go and finish writing my essay on Stalinist Russia. In a surprise cameo by my tear ducts, I felt moisture crowding behind my eyelids the other day when I was reading about the purges. I can't imagine. I don't want to.

11 p.m.

Sometimes I think the only reason Stuart is angling for Kathy is that he knows I am too. He's a smooth bastard. All reserve and broad-shouldered strength. He may well be my nemesis. And my antithesis! How about that?

Harvey out.

P.S. I have puny shoulders.
P.P.S. And I'm okay with that.
P.P.P.S. I'm not really.

October 5

Exhausted and a little in my cups. Worked four to nine this evening, training a New Little on the registers. She's one of the more interesting New Littles out of the bunch they just hired. Her name is Amelia, and what a funny little youngster she is. She demonstrates an advanced-level single-eyebrow raise. She's amusing—all frizzy-haired and fiery. I suspect she can, like, construct sentences and read books. Here's hoping she will go a little way toward Amelia-rating the vacuousness of her chain-smoking fifteen-year-old cohorts. (*Ameliorate*—get it? Oh, there's nothing like your own jokes, is there?) She's a healthy mess of contradictions. Sense of humor? Check. Very articulate for a youngster. She hasn't developed the ability to see past her own nose yet—takes everything seriously. Oh, adolescence, how much I don't miss you. She's smart and has reason to carry herself well. But she has this way of crossing her arms, gripping her elbows and looking down and sideways that screams "ill at ease!" to the world. Maybe all she needs is a good sensei to instruct her in the ways of, like, stuff. Maybe I'm the man for the job. Or maybe I couldn't be bothered.

I went back to Ed's after work. We missed the last bus and had to walk all the way, cutting across the park and freezing our arses off. Living the dream.

Kathy continues to lead the Field, and I am considering whether to bump sociology seminar Lauren from the list, as I've seen her walking around campus holding hands with a guy. Georgia from the deli is still a possibility, and probably up for it, and I may end up sleeping with her just to get Ed off my back. If he's so keen for Georgia to be put on her arse, why doesn't he do it himself?

"Time to break the drought, Chris," he said tonight. "Do you good."

"I'm working up to asking Kathy out," I protested.

He gave me the one-eyebrow raise—an advanced practitioner, like Amelia.

Yeah. The chances of Kathy ever having sex with me are slim to none. Ed reckons he's going to make sure Georgia comes out with us after work tomorrow night.

Harvey out.

Later

When my sister and I were little, Mum would read us a book called *Amelia Bedelia*. The title character was a housemaid who kept getting herself into "scrapes" because she was a bit of a literal thinker. She'd get really upset when she got into trouble and would run away. Actually, no, I think her employer got really angry at her and sent her away. Eventually and after much adventurous soul-searching she would come home. Her employer would greet her warmly, his earlier wrath forgotten, and ask her to make him some soup.

October 7

Last night I drank too much and bedded She's-big-she's-blond-she-works-in-the-deli Georgia at her place. Conversation was slim pickings afterward. I asked her if she liked Tom Waits. She said, "Tom who?" Enough said.

October 12

The timetable for exams and final essays is out. Six weeks until I'm all finished. It's going to take a superhuman effort to get all my work in on time and keep the credit average I need to graduate with honors in my new second major next year. Interesting. I'm going to work as many shifts at Coles as possible over Christmas break in the hopes of saving enough money to cut back to twelve hours a week next year. Maybe then I could put a little more time into actual study. Doing honors sociology and all, it would be nice to give that priority.

So, another year of school and then what? Too scary a topic. New paragraph, please.

Mick, Rohan and Suze will be waiting for me at the uni bar. It's almost dark out here on the lawn. I'd better go soon. I'm getting along quite well with a couple of the newer youngsters at work, both of whose knowledge of fruit and vegetable has blossomed under my firm but fair tutelage.

Donna is a very old soul indeed. She's fifteen going on

thirty-five and has a pretty fucked-up home life. Always keen for a drink after work is young Donna. She is Bianca's new girl pet; they're becoming thick as thieves, taking smoke breaks out the back together and all the rest.

The other one is Amelia. When my sister and I were little, sometimes I would piss her off so much she'd take a few steps back and then rush at me, fists raised. I would stick my hand out and plant my palm on her forehead, stopping her in her tracks. Her arms would flail about, getting her nowhere. She'd keep flailing until Mum heard the ruckus, broke it up and sent me to my room. For some reason I think of that sometimes when I'm talking to Amelia. She wears her entire personality on her sleeve. Upon (uncharacteristic) reflection, maybe I see some of myself in her. Zoe and I seem to have changed roles as we've grown older—these days it's me that tends to flail around while she stands composed.

Right. Beer o'clock.

October 22

The new youngster, Amelia, has acquired a bit of a cult following of late. Consisting of, well, me. It's relaxing to be in her company because there's no need for guesswork of any kind. I am going to try to push her in Ed's direction. A girlfriend would sort him out, I reckon, especially one that can read and write, and Amelia can certainly do that.

This will probably be the last time I write in this notebook until the end of exams. I will hardly have time to scratch myself over the next month, I have so much work due. But then it will be three glorious months of holiday. Consisting of three essential elements: beach, Land of Dreams and beer. See you in December. Provided I don't die from caffeine-induced heart failure, which, let's face it, is in the cards. It's late. If you'll excuse me, it's time for me to get into bed and look at the ceiling.

December 2

Welcome to the other side! I would say welcome to the season of love, but that might be a bit of an exaggeration, as will become clear when I get to the Field. Against all the odds, I got my essays in and sat my exams, proving for the third year running that there is a God and he loves me. My last exam was sociology—a three-hour nightmare. When the examiner said "Time" at twelve o'clock, the pen fell from my cramped fingers and I put my head down on the desk almost involuntarily. A curious montage of the year flashed through my mind, including lots of Michaela scenes from various stages of the whole sorry affair, watching Kathy holding court across the library lawn, fighting with my poor sister, who always seems to bear the brunt of my late-night seething, and, curiously, Amelia in the staff room at break, sitting on the chair with her knees drawn up to her chin, reading a dog-eared copy of Heart of Darkness and sipping tea from a Styrofoam cup.

Then I went to meet Mick, Rohan and Suze at the uni bar. Then I drank a lot. Then I went home and slept for fifteen hours. And here I am!

Right. Let's take stock. On the upside, I have three months off uni. On the downside, the Search for the Perfect Woman has still yielded no fruit, and I have no girlfriend with whom to spend these three months. I also have no money and will be working about thirty hours a week at Coles to rectify this. I will try very hard not to drink all my pay, but make no promises.

Rohan has finished his bachelor's in chemical engineering and applied for a job in Newcastle. It will be strange not having him at uni next year. He won't be around much for the holidays either because his dad is paying for him to go to Europe as a graduation present. My dad, on the other hand, has offered to make a contribution toward the board shorts I want to buy for the summer. A contribution, mind.

Rohan said he wanted to lend me his (parentally purchased) car while he was away, but his little sister kicked up a huge stink and he has to lend it to her now. I try not to envy Ro—the stuff his parents pay for, like the trip and the car, and the fact that he can spend so much more time studying because he doesn't work, while I get to take the bus to the Land of Dreams seemingly every goddamn day. I try not to envy him. It's disgusting to waste time envying those things when whole families, whole tribes, get slaughtered in their thousands in Africa, when leaky boatloads of refugees drown or starve in their hundreds in the open sea, and the children of those that do make it here have to grow up behind razor wire, watching their parents slide into insanity. When houses, families, towns get washed away in a day. I disgust myself when I covet things from Ro's life. But then, we humans have always coveted each other's oxen, haven't we? In Mod. Aust. Lit. last semester we were doing a unit on short stories and my favorite one was by Kate Jennings. In it she is talking about a fellow writer who enjoys phenomenal success and acclaim way beyond the modest (I assumed) success of the narrator. "Envy," says Kate Jennings, "is a grubby little emotion."

Anyways . . .

The Field is as follows:

—**Kathy** Look, usually I'd write "Token—never in a million years," but lately I seem to be gaining some mojo.
—**She's-big-she's-blond-she-works-in-the-deli Georgia** She's been trailing around after me a bit since the "Tom who?" incident. The youngster Donna from work seems a bit keen too. It may be completely unrelated, but Kathy has definitely been less withering lately. You never know your luck in a big supermarket chain.
—**Donna (token youngster)** Yeah, okay, she's only just turned sixteen, but, like I said before, she's sixteen going on thirty-five. She hangs out a lot after work. She never gets carded at the pub. There's a certain enduring appeal in a young woman who sports tattoos, holds a cigarette and a glass of Scotch in one hand, lights said cigarettes with a huge-flamed Zippo, wears more pieces of jewelry than you can count and can beat you at pool. Could I consider going out with a sixteen-year-old? It's a tough question. I'm pretty lonely and pretty desperate. Watch this space.

Yesterday I was standing at my register looking down toward the service desk at Kathy when Amelia piped up abruptly from the next register, "Hey, why does Gatsby love Daisy so much? She's a superficial skank." Then muttered more to herself than to me, "She doesn't love him."

She even takes the goings-on of fictitious characters personally. These are the things she thinks about when she is packing groceries.

December 14

Prepare for another well-lubricated sob story. It's that time of night, I've come home from the pub and you, like Coleridge's wedding guest, are as compelled to listen as I am to tell. Or maybe this is just drunken rambling that will never be read by any living soul. Even if my diaries are discovered after the apocalypse, people will trawl through the first few pages and say, "Who is this loser?" then, more importantly, "Who *cares*?" and chuck them on the post-apocalyptic scrap heap. Either way, I've digressed.

I had an odd experience at work tonight. It was about 8:45 p.m. and pretty quiet. I was chatting to young Amelia on the next register. At some point the chatting dwindled. She was tired. She'd been at school all day and it was the end of the week. She leaned both her forearms on the counter, bowed her head for a moment, then flung it up and exclaimed, "I'm starving!"

Instantly I was somewhere else.

I was in the one-room cottage in Leura, where Michaela and I stayed last March. Late afternoon, approaching evening. We are lying on the bed, the covers strewn this way and that on the floor. She is lying diagonally across the bed on her back. I'm lying with my head on her belly and one arm flung across her thighs. I listen to her steady breathing and watch the last patch of orange-pink sunlight on the wall fade, casting the room in dusky half-light. I take a deep breath of the skin on her belly, which rouses her from her sleep. She gently pushes my head aside, stretches luxuriously, then sits bolt upright and declares, "I'm starving!" She turns to face me. I push a lock of her teased-up hair away from her face. She bounds out of bed, pulls on her slip (birthday present from me) and sets about making a fry-up. I watch her. I love her.

Then I'm back at Coles, a little disoriented, but definitely back. I'm cursed with an extensive and detailed memory, so I'm no stranger to being laid low by a vivid Michaela moment. I try to get them out of my head as quickly as possible and am usually successful. But this was different. It was reliving, not remembering. The sights, the smells, the feel of the linen, the warmth of skin on skin. Real. Immediate.

Unsettling.

I'm going to sit out the back with my beer. It's after midnight, so it will be quiet, and there's a moon tonight. Our backyard is pretty unsightly and uninspiring, but on a brightly moonlit night even the rusty tin roof on the garage seems to gleam, and Eastlakes bathes quietly.

December 20

Work is getting crazy. Four more shopping days until Christmas. I had better get off my arse and do my Christmas shopping. I am tossing around the idea of whether to send Michaela a Christmas card or present or anything. I saw a pair of earrings that she would love in the window of a shop called Kashgar. Are you *crazy*, Chris? The bitch broke your heart and hasn't even called you for months! Sure, that might have something to do with the way you said—nay, *snarled*—something to the effect of "Don't you ever call me again, bitch" last time she called, but surely she realized that it was just the bleeding red mess of my heart talking?

Anyways, I'm off like a bride's nightie to meet the gang in the city for Rohan's farewell. He flies out tomorrow night.

December 21

I did a bad thing. I got home last night stinking drunk and singing the "Romeo and Juliet" song, rang Interflora and spent $400 on sending a huge arrangement of flowers to Michaela, *across the country*, mind you, with a very alcohol-induced Christmas greeting.

And all on my sleeping mother's credit card. When I came to this morning, I had vague recollections of doing it but hoped that it was just a dream. The credit card on my bedside table next to the phone indicated otherwise. I paid my mother back today, which leaves very little in my bank account. Fuuuuuuuck. Chris, it is high time you got over this girl.

December 24

Whillikers! It's almost midnight. Just got home from work, which was insane. Why do people always leave things to the last minute? I did too. Of course. I was in Go-Lo today during my lunch break buying crappy little gifts for my family with what's left of my money. I have very little remaining in the way of brain cells. What's everyone else's excuse?

As testament to this, dear reader, I did something this evening that I cannot account for. I finished my shift an hour before closing time and hung around for a while wishing people merry Christmas and the like. I seized my chance to kiss Kathy on the cheek. She didn't slap me or anything, which was nice, but that's not the unaccountable thing. I was chatting to Vic as she was marking down some bunches of flowers and sticking the REDUCED FOR QUICK SALE stickers on them. I looked over Vic's shoulder and saw young Amelia, who was up on register seven. While I was watching, she stopped scanning for a moment and wiped some sweat away from her temple with the outside of her wrist. The bloody air conditioner is broken. That's another story.

"Hey, Vic," I said, "I'll take one of them."

I wished Vic merry Christmas. Then my legs took me down to register seven, where I gave the flowers to Amelia. When I say *gave*, I mean I kind of threw them at her, mumbled something and bolted.

Go figure.

Anyhoo, Mum, Dad and Zoe are all out on the patio, having some relaxing ales after the frantic all-day Christmas preparations that I successfully avoided by being at work. Thank you, Land of Dreams! I'm going to go out and join them for what could be a rare moment of togetherness.

Merry fucking Christmas.

Harvey out.

January 15

The weeks are starting to blur. They consist of going to the beach with Mick and Suze, going to work, sinking a few coldies out back with Mum or Zoe in the evening, playing the odd game of tennis with Dad, reading my course-work texts for uni, reading the paper, staying up late watching crap TV, losing entire days to watching cricket and brain cells to the accompanying steady stream of beer. My dad and I live the cliché that men can't relate to each other on an emotional or interpersonal level so they do it through sports. When we are playing tennis, we are comfortably absorbed in the game, and the fingernail-scratching-down-blackboard who-the-hell-are-you suspicion that we usually regard each other with is gone. Because he is so much better at tennis than me, there is no destructive competitiveness. We both enjoy letting him give me pointers and he is chuffed when they lead to a slight improvement in my play.

Similarly, we can watch cricket together all day in companionable silence. No pressure to attempt conversations that are doomed to crash in a ball of flames. No speech whatsoever. We ask each other if we'd like another beer with either a grunt or a gesture. We quite happily occupy the living room together all day, day after day. If one of us has to leave the room or carry out some task around the house, he'll periodically call out for a progress report from wherever he is.

"Score?"

"Seven-fa!"

"Aaaahhgh."

"Clean-bowled!"

"Ooraahhgh!"

And so on.

January 21

Got a postcard from Rohan. He's on Mykonos. Having a ball. Just as well I am at a point of maturity whereby I'm happy that he is having a good time, rather than resenting his good fortune. He'll be back at the end of the month and has to start looking for a place to live in Newcastle—he got that graduate position he applied for. Of course he did. Some people seem to have their lives sorted out and are going about living them. And you know what? I'm happy for them. Really.

Nothing but
Interesting Times
April

Lonely Days Begone

The Land of Dreams is abuzz with news of an upcoming social event. Next Sunday after closing, instead of the usual trip to the pub that I almost always don't go on because of reasons well bemoaned above, everyone has been invited to a party at Bianca's house in Rose Bay. Her parents are overseas. Bianca's father, Chris confided to me, is the CEO of one of the big banks, and her mother is a "stay-at-home mum" despite the fact that Bianca is twenty-three. The three of them live in a huge harborside mansion, complete with tennis court, swimming pool and private jetty. Bianca's failure to go to uni, her part-time job in a supermarket and the various Coles slackers she sleeps with are, it appears, part of a larger framework of rebellion against her parents. I have no idea what that's about, but it does solve for me the mystery of how a twenty-three-year-old woman is able to support herself with a part-time job and spend most evenings out drinking. She doesn't *have* to support herself at all.

Bianca has always regarded me as one might regard a weevil in a rice jar, but I am invited to the party along with everyone else.

We're starting *Great Expectations* in English next week, having survived *The Bell Jar* and *Othello*. I am racing through it, which surprises me, because *David Copperfield* made me want to stick my hand in a blender. It makes sense to me that Pip falls in love with Estella as a child. Children don't know any better. But I find it hellishly discouraging—as well as fascinating—that even well into adulthood he is as obsessed with her as ever, despite her atrocious treatment of him. Don't we grow out of these things? She's just married some total bastard, and Pip's all cut up about it.

I empathize with him a great deal because a big part of his misery in the whole affair is that he never felt he could properly compete for her. No matter how much of a gentleman he becomes, to her he'll always be that poor, uneducated schlub from across town. He gets to live in close proximity to her and is the recipient of a bit of offhand titillation when she feels like it, but he never, ever has a real chance.

Like me with Chris. Will I always be the Youngster who can't shed her puppy fat, doesn't know what a bong is and has no fashion sense? This could go on for years. What if I can never free myself from it? What if I find myself forty years old and giving Chris marital advice with similar anguish?

The title character from The Great Gatsby (on the reading list for next term, but I read it over vacation) was in love with this girl Daisy for years and years even though she married someone else. Maybe not really love, but obsessed with this version of her that he had created. Boy, did he cling to it. He just couldn't see things for what they were. To the very end, when he dies from a bullet meant for Daisy's adulterous A-hole husband. In his beautiful swimming pool.

Penny has suggested to me a few times that I might like to get a grip on reality. You know, accept that getting together with Chris is unlikely in the extreme and stop torturing myself. I wish I could. It would make sense.

Our group at school is just starting to talk to some of the boys from our year in the boys' school. Not the real alpha males, of course, because our group is only in the middle third of the social ranking system. Sometimes they drift over toward us at lunchtime and brief words are exchanged, almost always with Penny. It's looking like we might even start eating lunch with some of them, and if we eat lunch with them, then that will logically lead to standing together at the bus stop after school. I might be able to find a more realistic target for my emotional energy.

But it's no use trying to stop loving Chris. That's my virus.

On the Friday before the party we have math for the last period of the day. I tell Penny that I'm worried I might have an aneurism or something if I don't get my lips onto Chris sometime soon.

"Man, my head hurts. It hurts; it hurts; it's going to explode."

"Oh, sweetie pie," says Penny.

"If he would just kiss me once, just once, properly, on the lips, I think I could die happy. If God would give me that, I swear I will never ask Him for anything else ever again."

"You don't believe in God," Penny points out. "And I guarantee that if you ever did get that, you'd want more."

I fold my arms and sulk.

As the day of the party draws closer, Chris seems to be less and less concerned with Sveta's thighs and more and more flushed with an apparent relapse of the Kathy virus. I can see it coursing through his veins, dilating his capillaries and pupils. He's hoping that this party will be the launching pad for a successful mission into "the Search for the Perfect Woman," as he terms it during evening break.

"You should see Bianca's place. Beautiful view of the harbor, the city lights. I can put my arm around Kathy and say, 'One day all this could be yours.' The sun will be setting. I'll have plied her with alcohol. It will be magic, Youngster. Magic will happen."

Magic. Kathy appears in the break room at that moment and starts to make herself a cup of International Roast.

He eyes her as you would a big juicy steak after a six-day hike eating only dehydrated vegetables. I know the look.

At the end of the shift, Chris and some of the other boys collect money to buy a few cases of beer for the party. Bianca frowns and says we can just drink her dad's liquor.

I begin to agonize about what I'm going to wear. The agonizing is short-lived, though, as the only casual clothes I own are jeans, T-shirts and boots. In cold weather I put a sweater on top. I can't buy anything to wear for the party, as I have a raging phobia of fitting rooms, and in any case I'm absolute rubbish at picking out clothes. Liza has been known to lend me an outfit, but she's taken them all to Bathurst. My mum is generally too exhausted after work to consult on such matters. Penny is about a foot taller than I am and none of her clothes fit me.

So I resign myself to the fact that my big decision to make is gray, white, black or navy T-shirt. In the end I decide on the navy one. It doesn't really matter, I tell myself. It's not like he'll have eyes for anyone other than Kathy. Pfuh.

On the day before the party Chris confides in me that he's decided to "throw his hammer at destiny" and make a grand gesture to Kathy, thus bolstering his chances for success the next night. The plan, as explained to me in the staff room, is as follows. He's been working on a poem for her for a week and reckons that tonight he's going to have it couriered to her house along with a bouquet of red roses. Anonymously. Then she'll have twenty-four hours to glow and to ponder over who they're from. By nightfall he'll have her down on Bianca's father's private jetty, with the harbor bridge and the city lights blinking across the water, whereupon he'll confess all and go in for the kill.

"Lonely days will be gone, Youngster."

"Great," I say, a little sourly.

He actually passes the draft of the poem across the staff room table and asks me to read it and give him my opinion. *The universe is against me*, I think as I read down the page. Incredible. Here I am, able to treat myself to the words of longing, desire and downright worship in Chris's funny handwriting, knowing that they are not for me and never will be. *Thanks, universe. Thanks heaps. You bastard.*

"Yeah, great," I say weakly, and hand it back.

On the day of the party there is lots of whispering throughout the store about the mystery flowers and poem that Kathy received the night before. After we close up at the end of the day, everyone gets changed out of their work clothes and we pile into various cars to drive to Bianca's.

I end up in Kathy's car with Chris, Street Cred Donna, Kelly and a checkout boy called Jeremy. There's not enough room for me to have a proper seat, so I have to lie across people's laps in the back. My head is in Chris's lap.

"Check it out, the Youngster lets her hair down," he says, giving my hair a playful yank.

I try to think of a response, but I can't.

Kathy drives like the grown-up she is. Her slim, bare arms turn the steering wheel gracefully. I'm not even old enough to get my learner's permit. I'm bloody Pip.

Chris looks like the cat that knows he's about to get a big dish of cream. I stare up and out at the upside-down trees whizzing past.

Bianca's family digs are indeed spectacular. The sunlight is low and golden by the time we are all set up on the deck with music and beers. The water is ablaze, and there is not a breath of wind. I can't help comparing it to the ramshackle little town house that my lot squish into.

Andy, Stuart Green, Ed and Lincoln are playing pool on the pool table just inside from the deck. Bianca, Donna, Kelly and Kathy sit together, uniformly smoking in their sunglasses and red lipstick.

I sit a little way from them with some of the other youngsters (dammit, he has me saying it now), including Sveta, of the killer thighs, and Jeremy. I gulp white wine and wonder when Chris is going to make his move. He is flitting from cluster to cluster, as he does at work, making everyone laugh, making everyone feel good. Bless him.

I try not to stare too hard at Kathy. Jealousy swirls around my irises, probably flecking the blue with green. How will she respond to what is about to be offered to her? The thought of her and Chris getting together for real parts my insides like a hot knife through butter. Curiously, though, the thought of her rejecting him and hurting him is almost as unsavory. I know Chris well enough to recognize him for the drama queen that he is, and I know that, in that event, he will take it hard. But having read the poem, I reckon the chances of her melting into his arms are pretty high.

What are you gonna do? I take a generous swig of my glass of white wine.

This is the first time that I have been in actual social proximity to Stuart Green. Stuart Green from Canned Goods and Vic from Perishables are the only two non-checkout staff that hang out with us, mainly due to their age and the fact that they both study at the same uni as Chris and Kathy. I think Stuart is about the same age as Chris. He studies chemical engineering. I don't really have a feel for him, as he has never said a word to me or even made eye contact. He only ever comes down to the front end of the store to talk to Kathy. There is sometimes a curt nod toward Chris, Ed or Bianca. He is generally unsmiling and a bit formidable, but incredibly self-assured. From the little I know of him, he is the complete opposite of Chris. Chris is inclusive and extremely social, and his speech is so laden with in-jokes, self-deprecation and sarcasm you have to learn to decode it. Stuart seems kind of minimal. He is a large guy, broad across the shoulders, attractive if you like cruel-looking men. And people do. Liza did once.

The other week, late in the evening shift, I'd heard squealing from down toward the service desk. Kathy was in a state of great agitation. It seemed that a mouse had run out from underneath a pyramid display of Vita-Weat. Three checkouts ahead of me, Chris quickly secured his register and started down toward the service desk. He was halfway there when Stuart Green strode out from aisle one, where he must have been stacking shelves. He carried a white polystyrene box, which he deftly brought down over the top of the offending mouse. With the mouse trapped, he put one steel-cap-booted foot on top of the box for good measure. Kathy breathed a sigh of relief. Chris had frozen in his tracks. There was a good few seconds when the three of them cut an interesting tableau. Kathy broke it first.

"Thanks, Chris, you can go back to your register now. We'll take it from here."

Chris looked from her green eyes to Stuart's cruel ones and didn't move. A couple of late-night customers had started to queue up at my register.

"Go back to your register, Chris," Kathy said, pulling service supervisor rank. "There are customers waiting."

Chris turned and walked back up to his register. He looked at me briefly, expressionlessly, as he passed. Stuart took care of the mouse. Somehow.

So right now at the party, Stuart is playing pool and Kathy is smoking on the deck. I'm chatting to Sveta about school when Jeremy comes up to us carrying a bottle of white wine.

"How's the evening going, ladies?"

He slots himself in between us and expertly pours three glasses of wine.

Sveta doesn't say anything. It's up to me.

"Fine. It's going fine."

"Cigarette?" he asks, fishing in his pockets.

"No!"

He stops fishing. "Cheers then. To Bianca's dad's Christmas bonus."

Again, Sveta doesn't say anything.

"Cheers," I say. We clink glasses and look out over the harbor.

Maybe it's the wine, which I'm not used to drinking, but I'm beginning to feel something resembling relaxation. If Sveta does kill men with her thighs, she certainly doesn't talk about it at parties.

It's turning out that Jeremy is an okay sort. Prior to the party all I knew of him was that he was a junior at St. Pat's and sold cigarettes to all the underage kids in the area when he worked at the service desk on Thursday nights. A lot of thin private school girls, I'd noticed. He does a roaring trade.

I'm doing pretty well at small talk with him right now. At least, for a social retard like me. He's a pretty nice guy. Cute in a hoodlumish kind of way. I ask him about his school.

"Yeah. I don't go a *whole* lot."

"What do you mean?"

"I mean, I just go when I have to."

"But . . . you have to go every day."

He laughs and refills my glass for me.

The only interruption is when Chris comes over, takes the glass out of my hand and suggests quite pointedly that Jeremy fetch me a glass of water. He seems to glare in Jeremy's direction, then leans down and says, "Ease down on the wine, Ripley, or you'll get a bit messy." Then he goes inside to talk to Ed.

I notice Stuart and Chris briefly glower at each other across the pool table. Jeremy returns with my water and another bottle of wine.

Around nine o'clock, I look round the deck and notice that Kathy is no longer on it. I peer inside to the pool room. Not there either. Hmm. Stuart, I notice, is also missing. Bianca has taken his place at the pool table. As soon as I fully absorb this information, my eyes seek out Chris. He has just come back out onto the deck carrying two strawberry daiquiris, fresh from the blender in one of the kitchens. He too is casting his eyes about the place, trying to find Kathy, then registering that both she and Stuart are missing. He sets the daiquiris down on a table, leans out over the deck railings and scans the garden and jetty below. Then he turns and walks quickly back into the house. The purpose in his stride and the uncharacteristic hardness of his mouth make me put my own drink down and rise to my feet. Jeremy stands up too and coaxes me to sit down again.

"I'd better just go and see where Chris is . . . ," I begin, then grab hold of Jeremy's arm to steady myself. I feel a bit wobbly. Maybe it's the wine, or maybe I've just stood up too quickly and got a head rush.

Jeremy sets his wine down and puts an arm around my shoulders to steady me.

"Chris is fine," he says. "He'll be back in a minute."

I deliberate for a moment, then detach myself and weave my way across the room with uneven steps.

"I'll be right back," I mumble over my shoulder.

Bianca's home is a bit of a maze, but after a search of downstairs I find a staircase. I take a deep breath before beginning the climb. I grip the banister firmly, definitely feeling a bit . . . something. . . .

Hold up. Quick, angry footsteps are striding down from the landing above. Chris bursts into sight, his face like the sky before a hailstorm.

"Hey—" I begin, but he leaps down the stairs two at a time, pushing past me so hard he'd have knocked me over were I not already clinging to the banister.

"Chris!"

Nothing. A door slamming.

I hurry after him to the front door, fling it open and run out through the front yard into the street. I can see him stalking away up ahead.

"Chris! Chris!" I run after him. At my second call he whirls around.

"Fuck off, Amelia!"

He means it. He has never, *ever* called me by my actual name. I stand there catching my breath and not daring to say anything else until he turns and keeps walking.

I'm sucking back tears when I hear the sound of glass shattering at the end of the street, followed by a distant "Fuuuuck!" in Chris's unmistakable voice.

A hand drops onto my shoulder and I hear Jeremy's voice saying, "He'll be all right."

I blink back more tears and turn to face him.

My head is a mess, whirring with questions, general disaffection and the hurt of being so rebuffed by Chris, who I'd walk across the Sahara for if it would do him any good. All of which immediately stops when Jeremy takes a firm hold of me around the waist and kisses me unflinchingly on the mouth.

Didn't see that one coming.

I break away for a second and say with all the eloquence warranted by such an occasion as my first kiss, "Um?"

Jeremy responds by kissing me again, very authoritatively.

I think, in quick succession: *What's happening here?*—*I should go after Chris*—*That's someone else's spit in my mouth*—*That's tongue!*— *Maybe I should stop this*—*Weird*—*Okay, that's not bad*—*Not bad . . .*

Jeremy interlocks all of his fingers with mine, gently squeezes my hands and stops kissing me. I open my eyes and look up at him. I can feel his breath on my lips. The seconds that we have been kissing are the first seconds in six months that I have managed not to think about Chris. Intriguing. And a bit of a relief.

"Come inside with me," he says.

"Okay."

He leads me back inside the front door by the hand. *So this is what it feels like to hold hands with a boy, I think. Nice.*

Instead of taking me through the house to the back deck, where the party is, Jeremy makes a clean left sidestep into a formal dining room with a never-used feeling. A huge and ornate dark wood table stands in the center of the room, flanked by glass cabinets filled with expensive-looking crystal and china. On the sideboard is the remains of the second bottle of wine Jeremy and

I had been drinking. But no glasses. He picks it up and drinks straight from the bottle, then motions for me to do the same. I swallow down a generous sip, fight off a sway, hand back the bottle and wait to see what will happen next.

What happens next is quite mystifying for a girl who spends hours of every day staring hatefully into the mirror and down at the scales. Putting his hands on my hips, he gently shepherds me over to the edge of the table. Then he bends down, takes a gentle hold of me around the thighs, lifts me up and sits me on the edge of the table. My shoes swing above the carpet.

More kissing—nice. Jeremy's hands are on my hips, pushing me, ever so gently, along the shiny wood toward the center of the table and then onto my back. He is on the table too and kissing my neck. I open my eyes and look up at the plaster designs on the dining room ceiling.

Interesting times, I think, a little foggily.

"All right, kids, that's enough for now."

It's Ed's voice and he's pulling Jeremy roughly off me. Jeremy made some protest until Ed said, "Your girlfriend's arrived, mate." Whereupon he vanished.

Oh crap.

That leaves Ed and me alone in the dining room. I quietly get down from the table. My head is spinning.

"Where's Chris?" I ask feebly, massaging my temples.

"No idea. But I don't think he'll be back."

"And Kathy and Stuart?"

Ed grimaces. "Still upstairs, I think."

"I feel sick," I say in a very small voice, because suddenly I do.

Ed finds a quiet place for me to lie down, then disappears to find someone to take me home.

Disgrace

I wake to my alarm the next morning, fully clothed on my bed and feeling absolutely wretched. It's Monday. School today and then work tonight. Summoning everything I have, I haul up into a sitting position. *Ahhhhgow.*

After a minute I stagger to my feet and stumble down the hall to the bathroom. My head pounds. My mouth is parched and foul-tasting. I struggle to remember the events of the previous evening.

And then it comes back to me. More or less. *Oh no. How did following Jeremy into that dining room seem like a good idea?*

I clean my teeth thoroughly and gargle with a generous quantity of Listerine. The foulness in my mouth remains. I fumble in the cabinet for Tylenol and then run a hot shower.

Leaning against the steamed-up glass shower recess, I wonder how Chris is faring. I'm going to have to see him tonight. And Jeremy. And Ed. But I can't think about that now. I just have to concentrate on staying upright, not throwing up and getting off to school without anyone noticing I'm hungover. Hungover! Me! I perk up a bit at the thought of telling Penny that I made out with a boy *and* got a hangover. I suspect there will be squealing on both sides.

Luckily there is an already ironed shirt in my wardrobe. With some effort I get dressed and pack up my school things and my work clothes. When I get downstairs, I can hear Mum remonstrating with Jess over some potty-related issue. I couldn't possibly eat, so I don't even bother to enter the kitchen.

"I'm late. . . . I'm off," I call to Mum.

"Oh . . . Bye, Amelia."

"I want my Dorothy undies!" I hear Jess shouting as I head for the door.

"They're all in the wash, Jess; you'll have to wear the stripy ones."

"No! Dorothy!"

I pull the door shut behind me. Looks like I got away clean.

My headache lasts for most of the morning, then subsides, leaving a general tiredness. I find that I am actually far from proud of the Jeremy thing, but I tell Penny about it anyway and skip immediately on to the Chris-Kathy-Stuart debacle. She takes it all in with a shake of her head and a big exhale, taking a cue, I think, from my general lack of animation. I sleep through the lunch period until Penny gently wakes me for science.

When I arrive at work, Jeremy is behind the service desk. I stand right next to him to check the roster—he doesn't look at me or speak to me and I'm not sure what, if anything, I should say.

"Hey, do you know if Chris is here yet?" I venture.

He looks at me for a microsecond, with what I'm pretty sure is a mixture of pity and distaste, and gives the briefest shake of his head. So that's how it's going to be.

I head to the locker room to put my bag away, wondering whether Chris will be too upset about the Kathy thing to come to work. Wondering whether Ed will have told him about my . . . thing with Jeremy. Until a bolshie voice booms at me from the doorway.

"You!"

Uh-oh. I turn to face the object of my desire.

"Hey," I say. "How are you feeling—"

"You!"

"What?"

He is still standing in the doorway. "You know what."

Holy crap.

"Do you think, Youngster, do you think that's any way to behave when you are a guest at someone else's house?"

"I—"

"Didn't your parents teach you any manners?"

I hang my head and won't look at him, although by now he is standing right next to me.

"I should call them and tell them how out of control their daughter is. Drunk and disorderly at fifteen!"

I abandon my contrite pose and bristle a little bit. "Look—"

"Is this the real Youngster then? Look out, world, here she is, ready to polish all your dining room tables with her back. A lick and polish as they s—"

"Hey!"

He cups his hands around his mouth and shouts, "Look . . . out . . . world . . . the . . . Youngster . . . has . . . landed!"

He's enjoying this. He's actually enjoying it.

"I turn my back for five minutes," he continues, "and you're fucking young Jeremy on Bianca's dining room table. They have to eat off that table, you know."

"I wasn't . . ." I can't bring myself to say fucking.

"Well, no doubt you would have been if I hadn't asked Ed to keep an eye on you."

I blush at the (hazy) memory of Ed's intervention.

"Jeremy fucking Horan of all people. I hate that guy."

"Well, don't you kiss him then."

"You are in disgrace, Youngster. Do you hear me? Disgrace."

I concentrate very hard on putting on my scarf and don't answer.

"Do you hear me?" he booms.

"Yes!"

"What are you in?"

"Disgrace."

"Qué?"

"Disgrace!"

"Damn right!"

He seems pleased with this.

"Did you know Jeremy had a girlfriend, the little shit that he is?"

"No, no idea—"

"How could you not? She hangs around the store all the time. The skinny one in the St. Lawrence uniform."

"They all look the same to me."

"He wears baseball caps backward! And you let him put his tongue in you!"

Now that is altogether too frank for me. I want to tell him "Steady on now," as my grandmother used to say.

"Well, I don't mind telling you that I'm frankly *appalled*, Youngster."

I don't answer, which fires him up even more.

"What am I?" he says, blocking the doorway that I had taken a step toward.

"Appalled," I say.

"That's right. I'm appalled."

"Well, good luck with that." I push past him and go out to the registers, knowing that the perfect comeback will come to me later that night as I am ironing tomorrow's school shirt.

No doubt it was Ed who squealed on me—he and Chris are best friends after all. Chris continues to ride me about the "polished mahogany incident," as he takes to calling it, for the rest of the week. I don't see him once speak to Kathy, though.

When I walk into work on Wednesday, Chris and Bianca are leaning against the service desk counter next to each other. I swear they both smirk when they see me.

"Well, well, well, if it isn't the Youngster," he calls as I scurry past. "Feeling all right there, sport?"

I make for the locker room.

"You're still in disgrace, Youngster! Got it?"

I studiously avoid making eye contact with anyone, especially Jeremy. I do glance toward the service desk, I hope in a subtle fashion, when this girlfriend of his is around. Chris was right—she needs a sandwich. And the cigarettes Jeremy slips her probably aren't doing her any favors. Whatever, like I care.

On Thursday at school, I bemoan the work situation to Penny. We are hovering at the edge of the grassed area, talking just to each other before we join the group. I don't think she quite knows what to make of Chris, or what outcome to hope for.

"He's being a bit of a jerk," she says warily.

"Yeah," I agree, and hurriedly add, "But he's not like that all the time."

She shrugs. "Mum and Dad are still making noises about me changing schools. They want me to apply for some scholarships. And take some exam to get into private school."

Penny's parents aren't happy about her school performance. She's not enthusiastic, they say. Her marks could be better, they say. She needs stronger guidance, they say.

If you ask me, Penny's lack of enthusiasm is one of the most glorious things about her. Example: she hates PE. No, listen to me—haaaaaaates PE. I'm pretty underwhelmed by having to put on a cringe-worthy sports uniform in the middle of the day, run around under the harsh sun until I'm red and sweaty, then get changed back into my school tunic (no showers) and be sticky for the rest of the day. But I do it twice a week, as required. As do the other girls.

Not Penny. She has never skipped PE, not even once. She shows up all right, with that unhurried, loping gait of hers, but instead of heading to the locker room with the rest of us, she slings her backpack down on the grass in the shade, sits down next to it, pulls out a book or magazine (always non-school-related) and starts reading. She doesn't wheedle to the teacher about period cramps or headaches. She doesn't forge notes from her mother. She just won't do PE. Ever. It's understood. Mrs. McGill never pulls her up on it and always marks her name off on the roll. It's just the way Pen carries herself. Like I said, gloriously unenthusiastic. And her marks are perfectly decent. I don't know why her parents are freaking out like this. Penny changing schools is a terrifying thought.

Everyone is a bit quiet at lunch on Thursdays because there is a double math period right after. People silently try to psych themselves up for it, and when the bell rings, no one moves right away. Actually, they freeze—like animals caught in the headlights of the oncoming juggernaut of trigonometry.

Sitting next to Penny in math, I notice that she now has two piercings in each ear, instead of one.

"When did you get those done?" I ask, surprised that she hasn't mentioned it.

"Last weekend," she replies, not looking up from her trigonometry.

"Where'd you have it done?"

"Did it myself."

"You WHAT?"

"I did it myself. With ice and a needle." She is still looking down at her bloody trig book, and I am flabbergasted.

I splay my hand palm down in the middle of her exercise book. "Holy *crap*, Pen, you could have given yourself blood poisoning! Why didn't you go to a pharmacy or something?"

She shrugs. "I boiled the needle and everything."

"What did your parents say?"

"I don't even think they've noticed. I did it when they went to a meeting with Jamie's doctors."

Penny's older brother Jamie is in his senior year and had some kind of meltdown a few months ago. Now he is living in an adolescent mental health unit—Banksia House, it's called. They have a school there and everything.

"Well, shit, Penny, I'm . . . surprised, I guess. Surprised that *you stuck a needle through both your earlobes.*"

She shrugs again.

After the final bell I make my way to work in a state of adrenaline-fueled anticipation mixed with dread. Maybe tonight Chris will cool off from the teasing and welcome me back into the fold. Maybe he'll have grown tired of it. One can only hope.

I walk into work and see him chatting to Ed at the service desk. He says hello in a perfectly civil manner and allows me to continue on to the locker room unmolested. All evening I brace myself for another barrage. None is forthcoming. The shift passes without incident. At nine o'clock I put up my CLOSED sign, pack up my cash drawer and set off to take it up to the cashier's office. I'm about halfway there when I hear Chris's voice over the store PA system.

"Attention, staff." His disembodied voice is business-like. "Ahem, attention, staff. If staff members have any hard surfaces in their homes in need of a polish, a member of the checkout team is offering her services in this area. She will polish wooden surfaces, plastic, glass, linoleum, ceramic tiling, even cork tiling, and will only expect a bottle of wine for payment. Bookings are essential, through myself, Chris Harvey, at the service desk."

I stand stock-still, clutching my cash drawer, a hot blush creeping up the back of my neck. Then I turn and walk briskly back to the service desk, the coins in my cash drawer rattling with each step.

There he is, counting out his own cash drawer, innocent as a newborn lamb. He looks up and regards me benignly.

"You don't have to book yourself, Youngster."

"Will you STOP this?"

"Settle down, tiger. You'll pop a blood vessel. It's all in good fun."

"Fun for who?" I bellow.

He looks down at the wad of twenties he is counting. It's maddening the way he won't even acknowledge that he is taking things too far.

"Why, why are you so pissed off about the Jeremy thing?"

"Like I said, it's all in good fun. You take everything so seriously." He drawls over the e in seriously, in the manner of one who is extremely put-upon in tolerating my adolescent spats.

I take a deep breath and do something brave.

"Why aren't you going at Kathy or Stuart the way you're going at me? That's what you're really mad about."

It's a good ten seconds before he replies, quietly and, for the first time this week, without belligerence.

"Because girls like Kathy eat guys like me for breakfast. And Stuart could and would squash me like a fly."

He looks gutted.

"Ah, Chris," I say, melting. "I'm sorry it went . . . badly. She must be out of her mind."

I wonder briefly if I could somehow broker a deal with God whereby if I put both my arms around Chris, his suffering would be transferred to me via skin-to-skin osmosis at a rate directly proportionate to how much I love him. But that's right, I don't believe in God.

"You know what happened, don't you? Stuart took credit for my flowers and poem and then fucked her on Bianca's parents' bed."

I nod. I'd figured.

"Can't you tell her they were from you?"

"No!" he says vehemently. "If she wants to be with a guy like Stuart, I'm not chasing her around telling tales about him. He's a mean bastard, though. Got his girlfriend pregnant last year and didn't want to know about it."

"He has a girlfriend?"

"Well, they're broken up now."

An awkward truce seems to be forming.

"So will you ease up about—"

"—the polished mahogany incident?"

I grit my teeth.

"Yes. Will you stop being such a prick about it?"

He smiles. "No."

"Jerk."

"Steady on now. That's no way for a youngster to talk. And the thing is—what are you going to do about it?"

I breathe out a large breath.

"Jerksville." But now I am smiling slightly.

"If you calm down"—he fits the lid on the top of his cash drawer with a decisive thwack— "I could be persuaded to accompany you to Rino's for a pepperoni extravaganza. I may even pay for it."

It is a school night and I haven't done my math homework.

"No more teasing," I say, not smiling anymore.

He looks at me.

"No more teasing," I repeat.

"Okay. No more teasing."

Special Treat

Chris buys a six-pack of beer on the way to Rino's.

"Special treat," he says, parting with a twenty-dollar bill. "You like beer, don't you?"

I hate beer. Hate it. "Yeah!"

Oh well. Love is pain. Or is it beauty is pain? I wouldn't know about the latter, but the former makes my sternum ache.

We pass a pay phone, which makes me think I should call home to tell them I'm going out for dinner. But then, it is after nine, so Mum and Jess will be asleep. Dad will still be up if he is back from rehearsal, but I doubt my lateness will cause any consternation there.

We sit in a booth at the back of the restaurant and order a family-size pepperoni pizza. My stomach muscles slowly unclench one by one as the relief of being back in Chris's good books floods through me.

He extracts a couple of beers from their cardboard pack and flicks off their tops with two satisfying hissing sounds. To the casual observer we must appear as . . . well, as equals, I guess. We are both wearing our work uniforms. I and I alone have Chris's undivided attention lavished upon me across the Formica tabletop. My cup runneth over.

"What shall we drink to?" he asks, pouring the richly glinting amber into frosted glasses.

I think for a moment, then raise my glass. "To the girls who eat boys like you for breakfast. May they suffer from severe indigestion."

"Right on, sister."

The honest clink of thick glass on glass.

"So, Amelia, what do you hate?" he says, leaning back in his side of the booth.

"Hate?"

"Yes, hate. You know, despise, loathe, abhor. What erodes you from the inside?"

"What, about myself, or the world in general?"

"Let's start with you, then move on to the world in general."

"I hate that I am fat and ugly and stupid."

Chris takes a swig of his beer. "You are none of those things, but I can dig irrational self-loathing. What else?"

"I hate that I want so many things I can't have. Just . . . don't like that sensation."

"What else?"

"I hate that I'm angry a lot of the time. It's exhausting. I hate that no one takes me seriously. I hate that I must sound like such a whiner right now. But, really, it's your fault for asking me."

"Hmmm. Yes, I take full responsibility. What about the world in general?"

I sit back in my chair and take a sip of my own beer. "I know I should say that I hate wars and starvation and inequity. And I do. But on a day-to-day basis, what I hate most is that both my parents smoke. Our house is small and there's only one living room where the TV and everything is. It smells bad, it gets into my clothes and my hair and I know it makes my asthma worse. My father actually gets angry at me when I complain about it. My mother just looks away and pretends she hasn't heard. The room gets hazy. They do it around my three-year-old sister. It really pisses me off."

"My sister smokes," Chris says. "But Mum and Dad make her smoke outside."

"I wouldn't mind if they smoked outside. But they act like it's *me* that's being unreasonable. When I was little, I made all these signs with red Magic Marker and stuck them around the house. SMOKE-FREE ZONE, SMOKING CAUSES CANCER and stuff like that. My dad made me take them down. That pissed me off too. I thought I should be able to express my opinion."

"By putting up signs around their house?"

"It's my house too, isn't it? And my lungs as well. And did I mention the asthma?"

"Dramatic much, Youngster? Maybe you'd have asthma regardless."

"Well, it will be pretty dramatic when they both get cancer. You asked me what I hate, and I really hate that."

"Anything else?"

"I hate that Pip still believes that Estella secretly loves him and that she'll come around one day. She won't."

"Are you still reading G.E.?"

"Three-quarters through. And Pip needs to grow up. It's never going to happen. He clings to this belief that they are not together because of cruel circumstance and because Estella feels that she owes it to Miss Havisham to do as she's told so she can't be with Pip, blah, blah, blah. When the real reason is that she doesn't love him, plain and simple. What's more, she's a bitch and she doesn't deserve him. But Biddy does. Biddy is a great girl and Pip doesn't even notice her. The Biddys of this world never get the guy." I pause for breath.

"Don't worry too much about Biddy. She does fine in the end."

"Don't tell me the end!"

"You're pretty hard on old Pip. You think he can just decide not to be in love with Estella anymore? He can just decide that?"

"I don't know. I guess sometimes it's"—I look directly into his eyes—"out of our control."

"Yep. I wish"—he breaks the gaze—"we could just decide to stop."

"Fancy yourself as a bit of a Pip, do you?"

"Maybe."

"Because of Kathy?"

"Nah. The Kathy thing is a means to an end."

"I thought you really dug her."

"I do. I did. I have for a long time. In a way. But the crux of the matter is that I'm seeking distraction from . . . well, from the real issue."

After a few swallows this beer doesn't taste too bad. I take a generous swig before inquiring as to the nature of the real issue.

"The real issue is that I'm in love with someone else. Actual love, not a crush that makes the shifts go faster and feeds my addiction to misery."

Well. I'd figured from the get-go that I had no chance with Chris because (a) he is too old, (b) he would never be interested in me in that way and (c) he has some jerk-off crush on vacuous Kathy from work, but now add (d) he's in "actual love" with . . . hey, with who? He didn't say who. Maybe it's me! Maybe he can't bear to tell me because . . . because he's worried my father would shoot him or something. I lean in and say, I hope casually, "Actual love?"

"You'd better not be mocking me."

"I'm not mocking. So why aren't you with this girl?"

"Was with her. Am not now." Again Chris has that gutted look that he does so well. He sort of looks down into his glass and then over my shoulder and into the distance, swallowing hard. He broods good.

"Anyways, Youngster," he says. "Moving swiftly on, you say that Pip should grow the fuck up and see things as they are."

"Well, yeah."

"Gatsby did that, right? He grew the fuck up at long last—realized that everything he'd hoped for was for shit, that despite all his elaborate efforts to be the kind of man that Daisy would want to hook up with again, despite all his longing and obsession, the object of his affection had chosen that Tom fuckwit and had no intention of leaving him. And then what did he do? He killed himself. So you know maybe it's better for Pip to keep this whole fantasy going in his head. Even being in unrequited love might be better than the cold hard light of day. He probably doesn't even know who he is without his Estella obsession."

"Gatsby doesn't kill himself."

"Yes, he does. He shoots himself and they find him in the pool."

"No . . . he gets shot in the pool by Wilson, who thinks that Gatsby screwed his wife and then ran her over with the car. Then Wilson turns the gun on himself."

"Good God, Youngster, you're right."

"There's no realization. He goes down to the pool saying that Daisy will call, to put the call through to him down there. Yuh-huh, Gatsby, that could totally happen—not. He dies waiting in self-deluded—"

"I think deep down, he knew."

"I think you are 'projecting,' as the headshrinkers would say. I can't believe I knew something that you didn't know."

"I knew!" he said sharply. "I just forgot that I knew."

The pizza arrives. We load our plates with as many slices as will fit, and Chris opens himself another beer. To my surprise I've almost finished mine too.

"So what else do you hate?" he asks between chews.

"How come you keep asking me that?"

"I'm interested. You interest me. I endorse your product."

No further invitation needed. I launch into my next pet peeve—perhaps a little less inhibited after the beer on an empty stomach.

"Well. I hate—I hate my mum—"

"You hate your mum?"

"No, no!" I say hastily. "No way. I hate my mum's despair."

"Her despair."

"Right." It's a struggle to express this one. I lean down to my schoolbag under the table, haul it up onto my lap and fumble around inside it.

"My mum has this really busy, really full-on job that she does Monday to Friday, plus she's got Jess to look after, plus my dad, plus all the housework and . . . she's really unhappy. The air in my home . . . is heavy with my mum's unhappiness. And her exhaustion. And her sheer dissatisfaction with her life. And I hate it. I can be up in my room when she's in the kitchen below and I feel her despair seeping up through the floorboards and into my room and throughout the whole house. You can hear her banging pots and pans, or cursing the vacuum cleaner. . . ."

"What's this thankless job that she does?"

"She's a high school teacher. English and history."

"Where?"

"Riley Street High."

"Shit. Tough school."

"Yeah. But you know, I've worked out what's really to blame for my mother's lot in life."

"And what's that?"

"Feminism."

"Feminism?" Chris raises one eyebrow. "Please explain."

I find what I was rummaging for in my bag—a tattered set of photocopied pages—fish them out and slam them down on the table.

"Well, our English teacher, Mrs. Cumming, made us read this thing called *The Feminine Mystique*, by some feminist called—"

"Betty Friedan."

"Yeah, that's the one. It was published in 1963 and—"

"Sorry, I need a judge's ruling on this—your teacher gave you *The Feminine Mystique* for tenth-grade English?"

"Yes."

"The same teacher that gave you *The Bell Jar*?"

"Yes. She's pretty wacky."

"I'll say! Continue."

"So, yeah, from what I can gather, Betty was writing about how after the Second World War there was this massive campaign to get women—"

"Middle-class white women, not women," Chris interjects. "That's who she was writing about really—she began her research on ex-classmates of hers from college."

"Whatever," I say impatiently. "She said women had been kind of herded back into the home and told that femininity equals being a "stay-at-home wife and mum." Apparently this lifestyle meant that most of them went insane with misery and developed Valium habits. Eventually a backlash movement developed called second-wave feminism, which tried to get the women back out into the world and not just be wives and mothers and dependent on men. And thanks to second-wave feminism, my mum spends all day getting shoulder-charged by a bunch of delinquent teenagers, picks up Jess from preschool, goes to the supermarket, comes home, cleans up the day's mess, gets the dinner on, gets Jess in the bath, folds the laundry, gets Jess out of the bath, serves the dinner, clears up after dinner, puts Jess to bed and collapses, waking up to do it all again the next day."

I pause for breath. Chris looks thoughtful.

"Well. I guess you have a point," he says. "It can *seem* like women like your mum got sold down the river by feminism, or at least caught in its wake. But really, don't you think they are getting screwed by patriarchy, not feminism?"

"I don't know. But before feminism, at least she wouldn't have had to do *everything*."

"Just the kids and the housework."

"Yeah. If she'd lived in the fifties, at least she could have had her Valium and her lie-down in peace once the kids were at school. She could have had a moment to read the paper and have a coffee in the sunshine. Maybe even see her friends. Go for a swim. All she'd have to worry about was how to work the latest 'vacuum-cleaning machine.'"

"Down with feminism!" Chris raises his beer in a toast.

"Down with feminism!" I laugh, and do the same.

"Seriously, though," says Chris, gesturing for me to wipe some mozzarella off my chin. "The Stepford Wife thing would totally suck if that was your whole life. It's not The Way. Let's not blame poor Betty for the sexual division of labor in your household. Speaking of which, where does your dad fit into all of this?"

"My dad." I stop chewing. "I'll tell you about him another time. I'm exhausted after all that—"

"Ranting."

"Right."

"Grade A ranting."

"Whatever. So what about you, Brutae?"

"What about me?" He raises one eyebrow, all film noir.

"What do you hate?"

"Well, I hate, you know . . . stuff."

"Stuff. I just bared my soul and you hate 'stuff.' "

"Betty Friedan and a dislike of smoking is your soul?"

"Cough up."

"Right now, Youngster, you remind me of a mosquito buzzing over what she thinks is a nice, normal, juicy vein, angling to swoop down, stick in the old proboscis and suck up some blood to take back to the kids. Little does she know that she's hovering over an artery and when she sticks it in, she will be exploded by a back draft of arterial spray."

On the Formica lies the now-empty pizza tray. My mouth burns from the spicy pepperoni. I am sipping my second beer and Chris is finishing his third. My watch says it is eleven. On a school night.

"Whillikers! It's almost pumpkin time," says Chris, gesturing to Rino for the bill. "You better drink up so I can walk you home, Youngster."

"I'm fine to go by myself. I do it every night after work."

"Can't have you walking home alone at this time of night. You shall be escorted."

"Righto."

I am getting nostalgic about this night and it hasn't even finished yet.

Outside there are chilly gusts of wind—winter is coming on fast. We walk through the dark, still streets, our footfalls and voices the only sounds.

"Will your parents be up?" asks Chris. "Should I prepare to field questions as to why I've had their prize-scholar daughter out on a school night?"

"Definitely not Mum. Dad might still be up, but he won't ask any questions. You don't have to come with me to the door."

For a while we walk in silence. Then with slightly lubricated daring, I ask, "So who's the girl?"

"Girl is Michaela. She went to my uni for a semester."

"And what's so great about her?" The darkness hides my pout.

"It's not something I can easily explain, Youngster."

"Pourquoi pas?"

"Well, we just . . . I . . ." He gropes around for words. "Look. Tell me to bugger off if this is getting too personal, but you've never had sex, have you?"

I gape in the dark. Should I lie? Would I score points? Would he see right through it? Maybe it would put me in with a fighting chance if he thought I had!

"I . . . no." Truthful old Amelia.

"Well, depending on who you're doing it with, you can go to this whole other place. Michaela and I went there. I haven't been able to get back."

We walk in silence. *Whole other place?*

"Why'd you break up?"

"She went back to Perth. From whence she came."

"And it was just over? What about the long-distance thing? My friend Penny's mum came over from the U.K. to be with her dad."

"She got back together with her boyfriend over there," he says stiffly. "He's called Brad, if you can believe it. Worst of all, on the day I put her on the plane home, I found out that they'd never really broken up. They were just on hold while she was over here. Believe me, if there was no Brad, I'd have moved to Perth as soon as I could raise the airfare."

"Crap," I volunteer sympathetically, silently thanking the powers that be for Brad.

"Certainly was," he agrees. "Is, I should say."

"Like Pip and Estella."

"Except that Pip never actually got his leg over." Chris grins through the darkness.

"Well. We don't think he did." I gesture for him to stop. "This is my house."

Coming to a halt, we face each other.

"Thanks for dinner," I say. "It almost makes up for the bastardry."

"My pleasure. I'm just trying to teach you to be a discriminate kisser."

"That's kind of you. Here I was thinking you were just being a complete A-hole."

"Tell you what."

"What?" I tighten and untighten my grip on my schoolbag straps.

"You welched on telling me about your dad. I welched on reciprocating a whole conversation. Here's what we do. We write each other a letter in lieu of the conversation."

"A letter about my dad."

"Yep."

"All right."

"Now. It's time you were in bed."

We slip through the front gate. Fishing out my keys, I creep up to the window and peer through a crack in the curtains. My father is reading in his easy chair next to the heater, a cigarette and a glass of Madeira in one hand and a copy of the New Yorker in the other.

"Good night then."

"Good night, Youngster."

I let myself in and quietly close the front door behind me. One of the tranquil moments from Liszt's Concerto number 1 in E-flat Major wafts through the living room door. One of Dad's favorites. It is nice.

"Amelia?" my father calls out.

"Yes," I call back from the hallway.

"Where have you been?"

"Dinner with a friend from work." I head toward the stair-case. Just before I put my foot on the first stair, he appears at the other end of the hall, still holding his Madeira glass.

"Good night then."

We regard each other.

"Good night, Da."

The First XV

I get to school every day in one of two ways. On nice days, I walk, which takes fifty minutes at a brisk pace. On crummy days, I catch the bus. Two buses, actually. One into the city, where I wait at Taylor Square among the social dregs of the night before for another bus to take me to school. That too takes fifty minutes, all up. Go figure.

This morning I take the bus. Standing alone at Taylor Square, I shiver in my thin school jumper. Penny and I are not on the same bus route. She lives at Maroubra Junction and comes from the opposite direction. There is a metal bench next to the bus stop sign that I sometimes sit on to wait. Today there is a homeless man asleep along its entire length. He wears tattered black clothing, his skin is darkened with grime, his long gray beard is streaked with dirt and in his sleep he cradles a bottle-shaped paper bag. With a cold gust of wind, his stench of filth, despair and illness reaches my nostrils. I move several steps away and shift from one foot to the other against the cold.

Later that day Penny and I sit on the grass among our group of friends, eating our lunch. We've always been a tight twosome within the larger group.

"How's Jamie?" I ask.

"A bit better, I think. But he's going to be there for a while longer." Penny draws her knees up to her chest, pulling the hem of her sweater down to her ankles. "Apparently we all have to go there for 'family therapy.' Mum's up in arms because she reckons it implies that she's somehow to blame for Jamie. 'It's not all about you,' I tell her, but it doesn't get me very far."

"You said that to your mum?"

"Nah." She smiles. "But I think it all the time."

I wish I had something to say in return. I offer her an apricot bar (the sugariest treat you can get at our school's health-food canteen), which she accepts, and we sit in silence for a moment.

The First XV rugby team from the boys' school is strutting out to the middle of the field. Wednesday. Scrum training day. Once assured that all eyes are upon them, they begin their warm-up exercise display. Bulging hamstrings are stretched languorously. Large shoulders are carefully rotated in their sockets, displaying to best advantage the pecs and biceps attached. The coach circulates, grunting encouragement and consulting on quadricep stretches and groin strains.

"Frickin' alpha males," mutters Penny mutinously.

Chris's lament that girls like Kathy eat boys like him for breakfast is still fresh in my mind. These boys don't eat anyone for breakfast—they don't have to. They are secure in their position. Only some junior and senior girls are allowed to approach them, and only after being given certain cues. They have parties where there are burly boys on the door to prevent any gatecrashers from entering. No one from our group of friends has ever been to one. Girls who are invited to these parties are handpicked. In my imagination, the parties involve smoke-filled rooms, kegs of beer, swimming pools, perfume and testosterone hanging heavy in the air, and pair after pair of folded strong male arms straining against their "fashion T-shirts."

Who is at practice today? I can see Ed Kennedy, Steven Harris and Jeremy Richardson. Luke Silburn, Monty Donachy and James Roberts. To name a few. The funny thing is how I know so many of their names. I have nothing to do with them. I've never even spoken to one. Yet somehow their names have seeped into the collective consciousness of the whole school. You hear whispers of their names along the corridors and across the school grounds at lunch. Information about which of them are dating what girls, who had a party last weekend, who was invited and who is casually mentioning that they went and did what to whom. I even know that Monty Donachy's first name is short for Montague. Go figure.

After warming up, the boys begin the somewhat comical routine of scrum practice on the scrum simulator thingy—a large hunk of metal that substitutes for the opposing team of hulking heads and shoulders. I wonder if there is a proper name for this contraption. They line up in formation and bend down to assume the position, arms around each other's arses and heads hovering close to the two pads in front. Then, with a terribly masculine Hunh! they thrust forward, all heads, thighs, arms and arses interlocked. The boys at the front have slammed their heads between the padded struts of the scrum simulator, and straining and grunting, they all push push push to move it back a few inches. Coach roars encouragement for a few seconds, then they all break away. Repeat the process. You lose track of how many times.

Every pair of eyes on the large school grounds, male and female, is unable to look away from this spectacle. Sometimes I think I can feel a silent alliance among certain groups who resent the privileged position that these meatheads occupy. To me, the whole exercise is just so visually ridiculous that I can't believe the whole school doesn't burst out laughing. But no one does. No one is brave enough to openly challenge the status quo. And maybe deep down we all hope to be invited to one of their parties one day.

The bell for sixth period sounds.

"What have you got now?" I ask Penny.

"Double art. You?"

"Study period. I'm going to write that letter to Chris."

"Ah. Well, if you need a break, come and wave at me through the art room window. I'll strike myself down with indigestion and need to be excused."

"Will do."

Dad

Dear Chris,

In the cold light of day, I'm not really sure what to write about. We just said a letter "about my dad," didn't we? That could mean anything. Plus it could go on forever, starting from my earliest memory of him and finishing with the manner in which he said good night to me last night.

I can be a pretty wordy lass (you may have noticed), but I seem to be struggling here. Let me tell you about my friend Penny's dad first. It might be easier for me to describe my dad by juxtaposing him with another one. Having been friends with Penny since seventh grade, I have had ample time to observe her dad. He works at your uni. He used to lecture in history, but now he does something to do with advising exchange students. He likes it.

When I first met Penny, I noticed that every day she'd pull out a lunch box. In it would be two sandwiches made with white bread, a piece of fruit and four crackers with peanut butter and margarine. Sometimes the sandwiches would be tuna, sometimes ham and lettuce, sometimes cheese and tomato, but the tomato was packed separately in foil so it wouldn't make the bread go soggy. She was often ambivalent about the crackers and let me have them. Eventually I asked her how come she always had this packed lunch—surely some days you just can't be bothered making it. I have those days. Or some days I'm running late and don't have time to make it. "My dad makes it," she said. And he does. Every morning he makes lunch for her and her brother, Jamie. Get this—when I sleep over on a school night, he makes it for me too!

One time I was sleeping over at Penny's and we were at the kitchen counter making brownies. Her dad comes in, puts an arm around her, hugs her, kisses her cheek and says something like, "What's my girl making today?" And when I've been over on weeknights, he kisses Penny's mum when he gets home from work. Like, openmouthed and with feeling. Did you ever see anything like it?

On the mornings when Penny's dad has to be at university early, he gives Penny and her brother a lift as far as the uni, and they join their buses from there. On the days that he works from home, he gives them a lift to the bus stop at Maroubra Junction to save them the twenty-minute walk.

On the weekend he potters about the house in overalls, fixing this and that, washing all the school uniforms and hanging them out to dry. Penny's brother, Jamie, plays on a soccer team—well, he did before he got sick recently—and Penny's dad coaches the team! Seriously. One night a week he and Jamie go off to practice at Lambert Oval and they play against other teams on Saturdays.

One night I was sleeping over at Pen's and we decided to go to a movie. Once there we decided to see a double feature and were home two hours later than we'd said. Penny's dad was waiting up in the living room when we got back and sprang to his feet saying, "Where were you girls? I was worried. You must call if you are going to be late."

It's not hard to figure out that these things made an impact on me because it's very different over my way. For starters, my dad is away a lot. He is a director. Plays, TV, film. One of the best. There is not a whole lot of work in Sydney, so he has to go where the work is. This means that up to five months of the year he is away, and it's been that way for as long as I remember. Directing a play in a different city, touring with a play, doing an episode of a TV show on location. Last year he went to Perth for three months at a time to teach at the Academy of Performing Arts, and he has a semi-regular gig teaching at a drama school in Singapore. When he is home, he's out rehearsing a lot, or in his study going over scripts and notes. Or worse, he's between jobs.

You'd think that when he's away, it would be harder for my mum, as she's essentially a single parent. But, in truth, there's less tension at home when he's away. As you might have gathered from my Betty Friedan "moment" the other night, my mum does almost all the housework, works full-time and takes care of my little sister, regardless of whether Dad is home or not. I help where I can, but I'm at work three weeknights myself now. I try to keep a low profile at home and not do anything that will (a) bring me to Dad's notice or (b) add to my mother's despair.

When Dad is away, the yawning inequality in the "sexual division of labor," as you put it the other night, is less obvious. When he is at home, I almost always feel angry with him and, it seems, he with me. So all our interactions—which are pretty few and far between in any case—are laced with anger. The ultimate insult comes in the evening, when he fills the family space with cigarette smoke. Well, they both do. Not only are they going to give themselves cancer, they're going to take me and Jess with them.

When I picture my mum in my head, she is coming in the front door at 5 p.m., holding Jess on her hip with one arm and a bunch of shopping bags in the other. She always looks tired. On days that I'm not working after school, I try to tidy up the kitchen a bit before she gets home, but more often than not she gets home to a complete mess.

Which brings me to how I picture my dad in my head. About a year ago, I got home from school, hot and sweaty from touch football, and dived into the shower. It was the first time in ages that Dad had been home when I got home from school. He was back in Sydney and preparing to cast a new show. I was in my room drying off and getting dressed when there was a sharp knock on the door and my name was barked out imperiously. I pulled on the last of my clothing and opened the door. Dad informed me I was to "put away the breakfast and lunch things" in the kitchen before Mum got home. Then he disappeared in the direction of his tiny study at the back of the house. *Breakfast and lunch things?* I thought. It was after 4 p.m. I toweled off my hair and slouched down to the kitchen. The sight that greeted me immediately clarified my orders.

On the kitchen table were the remnants of his breakfast and lunch. There were several dirty plates, a teapot filled with sodden tea leaves, a tea strainer bleeding brown into the pale wood, crumbs everywhere, some raw bacon rind, a heap of apple peelings, a dirty cutting board, a bread knife and the honey jar. The griller was open and displayed a layer of dirty congealed fat. In the sink were the three bowls that Mum, Jess and I had had our cereal in that morning, rinsed and neatly stacked where I had left them. I stood there, tasting my anger and outrage with an open mouth, wondering why on earth he hadn't as much as thrown out the scraps. Where the hell did he get off thinking that the women of the house existed to clean up after him? I leapt down the stairs two at a time and knocked on the door of his study.

When I was bidden to enter, I demanded to know why he hadn't cleaned up after not one but two of his meals, and why I should do it for him. My father is extremely quick to anger. His anger is one of the things on this earth that I really fear. It leaves me in no doubt of how powerless I really am. A minute later I was back in the kitchen, disposing of food scraps, rinsing crockery, wiping crumbs and oozing those familiar tears of impotent rage. That is the image of my father that dominates at the moment. Between that and my mother's despair, what do you do?

Thanks for listening. I feel like I could tell you anything. And everything.

Amelia

I debate whether to add a row of x's under my signature and decide against it.

Eighth and final period is math with Penny. The worst time to have math. Penny proofreads my letter for me.

"You know," she says, handing it back, "I can't remember what we used to talk about before you met this guy."

"Hmmm." I stuff the letter into my backpack.

After final bell, I get changed into my work uniform and hurry out to the bus stop with Penny. My bus has already pulled up.

"See ya," I call over my shoulder, running toward the throng. "Movies on Saturday night?"

"Um, I don't think I can this week. I've got a thing. Family…"

"Okay." I wave goodbye.

I squeeze onto the bus and ride to work, marveling that the aroma of teenage boy remains so pungent even though the weather is turning cold.

Chris is already on the register next to mine when I get to work.

"Check it out, y'all"—he punches the air in greeting—"Amelia Hayes is in da house!"

Bolstered by the warmth of his greeting, I walk, maybe even

strut, with uncharacteristic daring around to his side of the register and pull my letter out of my pocket.

"You requested a letter, Mr. Harvey," I say, "and I done brung." I slide it into the side pocket of his black cargo pants. Whillikers! I just pulled a move straight out of Street Cred Donna's book!

Chris stops scanning groceries for a moment and faces me. He smiles. It is a special, never-before-seen version of his usual winning smile. He fishes out some folded yellow paper from his other pocket.

"And for you, Ms. Hayes," he says, sliding it into the side pocket of my black pants and giving it the tiniest pat.

I back away a few steps and go behind my own register.

My eyes bore two holes into his back for the duration of the shift. At about eight, he turns around and bends down to retrieve a potato that's escaped from the scales. When he stands up, he winks at me and smiles.

Heaven help Amelia Joan Hayes, for she cannot help herself.

The Purple Notebook
(continued)

January 25

The workdays are long, especially when it's sunny outside. Ed and I have set ourselves the target of making up a new in-joke at the beginning of the week and having it instituted across the part-time staff by week's end. Young Amelia is the quickest of the lot, by a long shot.

There's this egotistical little shit of a checkout operator by the name of Jeremy. He's all of fifteen or sixteen and doesn't he reckon he's a player. He holds court down at the service desk on Thursday nights to a seemingly unending stream of private school girls. Sells them cigarettes, no doubt, and flirts like it's going out of fashion. Bianca flirts with him shamelessly, which fuels his ego even more.

I always thought that being completely superficial was mostly the realm of girls. I can see that Bianca, Kelly and, in my rare moments of lucidity, Kathy are pretty plastic when you get down to it. Jeremy is their male equivalent. I can't stand him. He doesn't have a pair of breasts to redeem him. After work I see him hanging around the food court with his skanky minions, wearing a baseball cap backwards—no shit.

Amelia is Jeremy's opposite. She's real. She's literate. I like her a lot. Or maybe I just like the idea of her. Because she's so young that she's out of the question, I can mentally make her into the Perfect Woman in Waiting. Is that what I'm doing?

Moving swiftly on.

Yesterday morning I started work at seven, helping out in Perishables until the store opened at eight. I worked through till close at nine, by which time I was climbing the walls. At five to nine, I was minding the service desk while Ed was out for a smoke. Bianca was busy making some careful adjustments to Jeremy's bow tie and gestured to me to do the closing message over the store PA system. It usually goes a little something like this: "Attention, customers, the time is now five minutes to nine and this store will cease trading in approximately five minutes. Please conclude your purchases and make your way to the checkouts. Thank you for shopping with Coles, the Fresh Food People." I sometimes wake up at night saying it. Anyway, I picked up the microphone, and instead of doing the closing message, I started belting out "Khe Sanh"—this '80s pub rock anthem about the miserable homecoming of a Vietnam vet. And I got as far as there being no V-day heroes in 1973 before Bianca wrestled the microphone from me and spat chips.

While she shrieked at me with Jeremy smirking behind her, the PA crackled to life again and Ed's voiced boomed through the store. He continued where I had left off for a good few lines until someone wrestled the back dock mike off him. Ed and I are as one.

It turned out there weren't any customers left in the store.

January 30

Rohan's back from Europe. Going to the pub with him, Mick and Suze. Now.

February 8

Uni resumes in three weeks. Rohan has found an apartment in Newcastle and we are going up for his housewarming party next week. He starts the new job in two weeks. I'm still working twenty-five to thirty hours per week at Coles, but really hope to cut it down to twelve when uni begins. Zoe has also found herself a graduate position at an accounting firm in the city, and Dad is chuffed. She reckons she's moving into her own place as soon as she saves enough money for rent and furniture. Good for her, I say. She hasn't told Dad and Mum about this plan. Dad will freak out big-time and say she should stay at home until she can buy her own place. "Why throw your money away on rent?" is his standard response. I see the payment of rent more as an investment in your own sanity and independence.

February 14

I'm writing from Rohan's flat in Newcastle. The party is tonight. He, Mick and Suze have gone off on a final ice-and-tea-light-candle-buying mission. I begged off and have set myself up on Ro's bedroom balcony with a beer. I can see glimpses of the harbor. There are several big tanker ships moored way out to sea, patiently (it looks like) waiting for their turn to come into port. I wonder how long they have to wait. I wonder what the crew members do while they are waiting. In my imagination, they are playing cards. Opposite Ro's block are six huge old town houses, complete with five-pot chimney stacks on every seam. They're beautiful. It's a quiet street. It won't be tonight.

We drove up yesterday—Suze, Mick and me—in Mick's dad's 1987 Land Cruiser. What a beast. After the usual painful crawl along the Pacific Highway getting out of the city, we let loose on the F3, turned up the music and gunned it to Newcastle. As we were driving down and then up the gully with those two huge wind socks, I had one of those moments when you get nostalgic about something as it's still happening. Anticipatory nostalgia. We were driving fast. Somewhere around the Peat's Ridge exit I had ferreted out one of Mick's Kings of Leon CDs and we were chatting and singing by turns. Suze took the album jacket cover out of my hands and studied it. "They are some tight pants," she said to no one in particular. "Yessir, they are." We descended the gully, our heads flung back, singing at the top of our lungs. And then coasted up the other side on the speed we had picked up on the way down.

Years from now, when Mick, Suze, Rohan and I have all grown up, dispersed to the suburbs with our spouses and children, chins sunk deep into collars on the Long March of the fifty-year mortgage and hardly ever seeing each other, I will be going through some boxes of old CDs and will come across that Kings of Leon album. I will put it on and be hurtled back in time to the day when I was fanging along the F3 with my mates Mick and Suze, singing so loudly our voices cracked, on our way to Ro's housewarming party in Newcastle.

And what an event it promises to be. The Jell-O shots are in the fridge. When the ice arrives, we will mix up a giant bowl of Blue Lagoon. There are three cases of beer waiting to go into the bath. We've ordered a heap of Turkish pizza to arrive at about eight and got chips and dips to last until then. Heaps of Rohan's engineering friends are coming, including the lovely Stella, who is impossibly petite and pretty for an engineer. Get this—she is now studying for a master's degree in chemical engineering, after which she will be able to call herself a master brewer. Is there anything cooler than that? Is there?

Ro's cousins and their friends from up this way are coming, and some other mates from uni might make it up too. Maybe the Perfect Woman is somewhere not too far away, standing in front of her wardrobe, flushed from the shower and clad in a bathrobe as she chooses what clothes to wear tonight. Godspeed, Perfect Woman.

It's hot, damn hot. High nineties. We spent the morning on Nobby's Beach, surfing and throwing the Frisbee, but had to hot-foot it out of the sun by eleven. Literally hotfoot it—the sand was too hot to walk on.

I'll wrap it up now. I want to rock back on my chair and absorb the view. Thumbnails scraping at the label of my beer. A little black tugboat is chugging out to meet a tanker. There's a grand old cathedral up the road—I can see the spires. The bells are ringing.

5 a.m.?

There are traces of orange in the east.

> Alone, alone, all, all alone,
> Alone on a wide wide sea!
> And never a saint took pity on
> My soul in agony.

Please God don't let me puke.

February 15, 11 p.m.

Back in my own bedroom. Tonight is my first alcohol-free night in I don't know how long. My stomach has just protested at the mere mention of alcohol—oops, sorry, stomach, I mean the a-word. It was a subdued drive back to Sydney. I don't know who among us was more hungover. We all looked as rough as guts. Uncle Jeff was here for dinner when I got back and wanted to start something with me. As usual, he initially disguised this as seemingly innocuous chummy inquiries about my life or my opinion of some current affair. I offend something that runs deep in Uncle Jeff. More so since his divorce. Or maybe his divorce just coincided with when I started to grow a personality.

Anyways, I made excuses of feeling unwell and stumbled straight out to my bedroom. Aspirin, ibuprofen, Tylenol, bacon and eggs, tea, coffee—none of them can fix the pain at the base of my skull, the taste in my mouth or the general indignation of my internal organs.

I may have gotten a bit messy last night, as evidenced by the scribbling of what appears to be a verse from *The Rime of the Ancient Mariner*. Needless to say, the Perfect Woman was not in attendance at Rohan's housewarming party. Some of Ro's mates came to the party at about midnight, having been to see a band at the uni bar. In my lubricated state, that got me to thinking about what I had been doing a sterling job of not thinking about for the whole trip. Namely, the one time I had been to Newcastle before.

Just after midyear exams last year, Michaela and I came up to stay with a friend of hers who was doing a semester at Newcastle Uni. A "Perth girl." There's a whole Perth thing. They all seem to know each other. Like a big country town. I digress. We came up to stay with this friend in her giant share house. Student share houses always fascinate the likes of me, who have to live at home if we want to keep studying.

Bernadette, this friend of Michaela's, lived with eight other students. There were two big living rooms, with coffee tables made from milk crates and huge, tired-looking Tarantino posters on the walls. We slept on the floor of her big, damp bedroom with peeling wallpaper and rotting carpet. We had a big barbecue out back with a bunch of other students on Saturday afternoon. We went to the uni bar to see some indie rock band. It was three weeks until Michaela was due to go back home. I was dreading her immediate absence, but I didn't think for a second that we would be over when she went back. Pretty much the only time we weren't touching was when one of us went to the toilet. This bordering-on-desperate grip was mutual—she must have been holding on for all she was worth, knowing that soon she'd be going back to Brad, and wondering how on earth she was going to play that one.

In retrospect, I can see that Bernadette was a bit uncomfortable and bemused by all the coupliness. One time she and Michaela were in the kitchen and I overheard her ask in a low voice, "Have you spoken to Brad lately?" and Michaela reply, "Um, yeah. Last week." They both started, almost imperceptibly, when I came into the room.

"Who's Brad?" I asked.

"A friend from back home," Michaela replied without missing a beat.

"There are real people called Brad?"

"At least one." She smiled in my direction but didn't look at my eyes. "Cup of coffee?"

At the gig we were one of Those Couples. You've seen them at every gig you've been to. They stand oblivious to the many petty insults of being surrounded by a sea of buffeting, drunk people. Usually the guy is standing behind the girl, both his arms encircling her, almost supporting her weight and protecting her from the crowd. They whisper in each other's ears from time to time. The bloke will often tap-tap along with the music on the girl's hips.

And they are so going home to get it on after the show. You know it and I know it. Anyways. That Couple was me for a few months.

Later that night I woke, on the dusty floor of Bernadette's room, to find Michaela propped up on one elbow, studying me while I slept.

Alone on a wide wide sea.

February 28

Ed was more or less lucid at work yesterday, so I took the opportunity to make a couple of suggestions. One—he should cut down on his pot. Two—he should ask out young Amelia. She's not even three years younger than him and she's a great girl, all of which I pointed out. She's smart, she'll make you laugh, I said. She's cute, she's straight down the line, I said. You'll have a good time with her, I said.

Ed shrugged and made noncommittal noises.

"What? What?" I pestered him. "Why not?"

He put down the crate of receipt rolls he was carrying and leveled with me. "Chris, she's a very nice girl. But I'm not quite the fan that you are." Well. His life. At least I gave Georgia from the deli a go!

March 3

Okay. Let's take stock. I'm working only fifteen hours per week, so am more or less on top of uni work at this early stage in the game. This morning I didn't start till eleven, so when I dragged my arse out of bed, everyone was at work. A magazine article titled "Are

You Drinking at Problem Levels?" just happened to be open on the kitchen bench. Mum and Zoe are in unsubtle cahoots.

Let's take a look at the Field:

—**Kathy** The Kathy virus has been in and out of remission for, let's see, three years now. I might make an executive decision sometime this year to actually hit on her proper and see what happens. Kathy reserves the right to shoot me down in a ball of flames at all times. At least I'll go to my grave knowing that I did not go quietly into that good night.

—**Stella the master brewer** The pretty engineer. Although, I noticed her and Rohan doing some close-talking at his housewarming. Perhaps I should sound it out with him before I ask Ro for her number.

—**Sveta Tarasova (token youngster)** Sixteen-year-old checkout operator. Perfectly legal. Amazing legs. Trained her up with my own hands. Bet I could have her on her arse in a matter of coffee dates. They all seem to look up to me with starry eyes, the youngsters. I excite them. I wish I was as irresistible to the Kathys and Michaelas.

March 15

There was a fire in the Wonder Bread factory last night. Thousands have been left breadless. Foul play is suspected.

March 18

It's Sunday night. Uncle Jeff was here when I got home from work this afternoon and was obviously staying for dinner. He and my parents were sitting out back under the awning. The empties from a six-pack of beer were lined up along the kitchen counter. Crap. I skulked about in my room and pretended to be doing uni work until Mum came in and said I had to come out and talk to him. It is SO humiliating when she does that. I'm one-and-twenty years old. I can vote, enlist, drink legally in the US and "come into" my inheritance in a Jane Austen novel. But I can't come home from work and flop onto my bed in peace if I choose. It's all wrong. God, I wish I could move out. If I dropped out of school and went full-time at Coles, I could start looking for a place after a month's pay. The Perishables manager would have me full-time in a heartbeat.

So out I come to talk to Uncle Jeff, who is my father's brother, older by five years and the worst kind of baby boomer. He's an environmental manager or some such. No one knows exactly what he does. He worked for years and years at the Department of Infrastructure, Planning and Natural Resources. Then he left there to work in the "private sector." He and Aunty Jo used to live in Lane Cove with my two cousins. After the divorce, he moved to a flat in Rose Bay, where he has remained. His barely veiled anger toward me also extends to "my generation," whatever that means. I suspect that Uncle Jeff rides his angry wagon in my direction because his own kids chose to live with their mother. Today—predictably—he expostulated about how "my generation" is apathetic and never protests about anything.

"Yes . . . ," I said. "Well . . ."

My mother shot me the pleading look. Let it go, son.

"When I was a student," Jeff continued, "we got out there and protested about the things that mattered. We made our opinions known. We put in the hard yards. We effected change." He paused for breath and looked pleased with himself.

"You raged against the dying of the light," I added helpfully.

My mother looked uncertain and Jeff looked undecided.

"Chris, you have an essay due, don't you?" Mum was giving me an out, knowing there was only so long I could hold the line.

"I do."

"Well, you can be excused to go and work on it."

"What's it on?" Uncle Jeff piped up, louder than necessary, in all his belligerent glory. "Bloody poofterdom in John bloody Keats?"

Oh, good times.

I put in the hard yards, I thought, back in my room. *I just put them in at the Land of Dreams.*

April 2

Bianca's having a party at her parents' place. Waterfront home on Rose Bay. I've been there a few times before. You could swim out to Shark Island.

It's time I threw my hammer at destiny and put my case to Kathy. The Kathy virus is hard to understand. Is it just because she is beautiful and uninterested in me? Is it just the chase? The masochistic thrill of the threat of being rejected? Coupled with me being lonely and rootless? Whatever it is, it's pretty strong and has been going on for long enough. Time to act—and then at least I'll know. After some careful mustache-twirling consideration, I have devised the following plan.

At uni she seems to be surrounded by rather dull types who, nevertheless, have a pretty good future earning capacity—doing commerce or engineering (hello, Stuart Green!). I think my only in is to play up my sensitive liberal artsy side. Juxtaposing myself with the dullards may work in my favor because, although she knows and I know she will one day choose one of them to provide for her future, she may like to go slumming with the sensitive guy prior to that. You know, just to have had that experience. Years from now, she can look out over her neatly clipped lawn and ocean view while her children are wolfing down their dinner and remember an affair from days of yore—Christopher Harvey, who wrote her poems and made love to her with such passion. She'll wonder where he is now. I wonder where I will be then. Probably in the Perishables department at the Land of Dreams.

I'm getting ahead of myself. Again.

I'm going to write her a poem. I've had the makings of one in my head for a while, so I'll pen it tonight. Then, the night before the party, I'll send her the poem and some flowers, but I won't let her know who they're from. She'll have all night to lie awake and wonder about the identity of the passionate wordsmith. Then, the next evening at Bianca's party, I'll take her aside, and bam! Confess! Give her the full voltage of my charm and persuasion.

Now all I have to do is write a poem.

April 9

Here is the current draft of the poem that will hopefully turn the Kathy virus into friendly bacteria:

> The sun has set the ocean ablaze
> With gold and pink,
> A million dancing sparks.

It shines because you smiled.
In its warmth I regard
The colors of your face,
So young, and yet old.
Eyes bright green, like a shallow beach
On a sunny day, and ringed
With the darkness of a pine forest.
For years I have loved these eyes,
Longed to find their favor,
And kiss their lids.
In their center lies the promise of a deep
And dreamless sleep.
Mottled clouds scud across the sky,
To smother the sun.
They came because you frowned.

If this doesn't get me somewhere, and fast, I will accept that the universe is denying me this particular prize and turn my attention to a new futile exercise.

April 16

The poem and flowers were a hit. What a brilliant idea! A stroke of genius in the field of romantic endeavor! The only sour note in the evening was that before I had a chance to make my confession, Stuart Green stepped up.

I'm sure Kathy would have melted into my arms had she not been too busy having sex with Stuart Green, who took credit for my flowers, took credit for my poem and then took Kathy upstairs.

There is no justice in the universe. I have suspected this for a long time, and now I think no other conclusion can be drawn.

And to add insult to serious narcissistic injury, young Amelia went and hooked up with that mid-teen power tool Jeremy Horan. I had her billed as the antidote to Daisy from *The Great Gatsby*. I thought she represented the ultimate triumph of good over evil. With all her ranting and posturing, she gave me the impression that she really stood for something. I'm not sure what exactly, but definitely something. She's smart. But all he had to do was pour her a few generous glasses of wine and put in an hour of conversation.

I am working tonight and she will probably be there. I feel it incumbent upon me to teach her better behavior. How is it that guys like Stuart and Jeremy are rewarded for their fuckwittery? If someone like Amelia goes for someone like Jeremy Horan, we may as well all pack up and go home. Shit! Land of Broken Dreams.

All right, I'd better do some study now.

The Field is as follows:

Yeah, no, I didn't have to run away in the middle of the entry or anything. I was just using the blank space as a device to communicate that there are NO options at the moment. Arty, no?

Amelia is going to rue the day she let that boy's tongue any-where near her. I'm going on the rampage.

April 19, midnight

Midnight was the "witching hour" in The BFG, I seem to recall. My mother read it to Zoe and me when we were small. I remem-ber Sophie peeking between her curtains at the orphanage to get a glimpse of the streetscape "now the witching hour was at hand." Everything looked eerily askew and milky...and then! She catches her first glimpse of the BFG down the road, wearing his dark cloak and carrying his dream-blower. Zoe and I gripped each other's hands under the covers, as terrified as Sophie.

I just got back from a thoroughly enjoyable evening in the company of Amelia, whose cult following is gaining momentum. If I were less of a prick, I might feel a bit guilty about the way I've been torturing her this week. But I think we all learned some-thing. I took her for pizza after work and let her drink Big Girl drinks. I know, I know, but if I don't lead her astray, who will?

Somehow I ended up telling Amelia about Michaela. I really must have forgotten that she is a youngster and should be treated as such. Being the gentleman I am, I walked her home. When we got to her house, she peeked through the front curtains before letting herself in. That's what reminded me of Sophie from The BFG.

I really like talking to her. I like how she turns everything over and over in her mind, and that she doesn't censor herself. Being with her is easy. I seem to laugh.

Apparently I owe her a letter. A short piece titled "What I Hate." I caught the last bus home and have poured myself a (generous) nightcap. I'm just going to sit here for a while. I'll write the letter tomorrow.

1 a.m.

If she were even just two years older, she'd be leading the Field.

1:30 a.m.

But she ain't.

2 a.m.

I'm going to let the Jeremy thing drop. She's only a little 'un. Didn't know any better. Plus she might start to fight back.

April 26

It's cold in the mornings and evenings, but warm during the day. Harder to get out of bed in the morning. Do you know, I may have slightly reduced my nightcapping? Maybe Rohan moving away has something to do with it. I still see Mick and Suze often, but not as much as last year. We have been somewhat diminished by Ro's absence. Plus we sort of relied on his car a lot of the time. Mick and Suze live in the same suburb, so it's easier for them to see each other.

I haven't gotten completely trashed for about two weeks now. It's strange. I was thinking this morning that without my constant stumbling about, headaches, crankiness and general misery over Michaela, would I even recognize myself? Would I be boring?

Shit, maybe I should get wasted tonight. Tomorrow is Saturday. I'm working all day, as are most of the others. Afterward, we'll go to the pub. Ed and I will watch Fox Sports, play pool against Bianca and Donna, drink beer and then be four hours older. Same old. Rohan had the right idea. How long can you stay in one place for? My life just reminds me of Michaela. I think I need to get the fuck out of here. I need to see a new streetscape. I need to have a routine that isn't five years old. I need to have my own place to live and to forge a path that belongs to me.

I'm resenting the fuck out of both my parents lately, and neither of them are bad people. I just don't want to be the son-living-under-their-roof anymore. I don't want to be told to come out of my bedroom and talk to Uncle Jeff, or whoever they've got over on any given day. Or my dad knocking on my bedroom door. *'Bout time you gave that lawn a bit of a mow, son.* I'm not denying that the lawn needs to be mowed or that it's fair I do some jobs around the house. I just hate it when he tells me what to do; I'm an adult, for God's sake!

If I had my own place, it's likely that I would still choose to see Mum and Dad often—I love them. But it needs to be on different terms than the ones that exist while I'm living here. The end of this year can't come soon enough. Bring on the next phase! Again, I'm jealous of Rohan. He chose a course that would clearly lead to a job after uni; he got one, and now he gets to have his own flat in Newcastle. What am I going to do with a degree in sociology? Even if I could afford to, I don't want to go straight to grad school. I need a break from study. Whatever will become of me?

April 28

I'll write my letter to Amelia now. Here goes.

Dear Youngster,

What I hate could fill a book, and maybe one day it will. Here is a concise version.

1. Oh-Brad. I have no idea what he looks like, but in my mind he is tall, broad-shouldered, cut, tanned and handsome. Also, I imagine that he is finishing some degree that will lead to an extremely well-paid job. Every day of his life he has unfettered access to the woman I love. But the worst thing is I know Michaela well enough to know that, surely, she wouldn't have lied and lied and then thrown me over if she didn't love this guy. I won't even say "dumped me for Brad," because if she never broke up with him, then she and I were never really together.

2. Stuart Green. Stuart Green represents all that is unjust in the universe. The world is there for him to plunder, as far as he is concerned. This attitude rakes in the spoils. I used to think that behind his eyes lay an expanse of soulless

nothingness. But in the last year I've changed my mind. Behind his eyes lie gusts of well-disguised malevolence. He's set a new low with the Kathy thing.

3. I occupy a strange kind of life-stage purgatory at the moment. I'm twenty-one, but I live with my mummy and daddy, in my childhood bedroom. I won't be considered "independent" by law until I am twenty-five. Please, God, let me be well out of here by then. Anyway, Youngster, it's a particularly powerless existence that I eke out at 16 Acacia Terrace and it's making my relationship with my parents crapper than what it should be. Watch this space. Which brings me to my next point.

4. As soon as I finish uni, I'm moving out. If needs be, I'll increase my hours at Land of Broken Dreams to cover my rent. Somewhere affordable but not at the ends of the earth. Who knows what is in store for me on the "career" front, but at some point in my twenties the chorus of prompts from my father, my uncle and various other players to buy property will reach

a crescendo. "I bought this house when I was your age," "Renting is dead money," etc., etc. See, Youngster, I regard rent payments as the price of independence, not dead money. Do they really think it's fair to compare Dad buying our three-bedroom house in the seventies for $24,000 to the task of buying a three-bedroom house in any decent suburb today for a minimum of $600,000? And with student loans to boot. I get anxious just thinking about it. All this you have to look forward to, Youngster.

5. I covet my neighbor's oxen. I'm not all happy for people who have their lives sorted out and go about living them, who have money, independence, intelligence, influence and hot, hot girlfriends. My mate Rohan rang the other day and said he's putting down a deposit on a house in Merewether, which is a suburb in Newcastle. He's only been working for two months. "How'd you come up with the deposit?" I couldn't help but ask, knowing the answer. "My dad." Right. Of course. Good for you, Ro. Disgusting, aren't I? I'm not going to give you any more examples because I don't want you to think the less of me. Bottom

line is—I can't run my own race. I'm constantly checking what's happening in the other lanes.

b. I'm young; I'm (at least kind of) healthy; there is a roof over my head, food on the table, heat in the house; I have friends; I have access to a college education; I live in a safe city with clean beaches—and yet I'm miserable. I spend most of my time massaging my temples or fuming about a range of grievances. If you'll excuse me, I'm going to wrap it up now so I can watch the patch of sunlight on my bedroom wall fade as the sun slowly sets, casting the room in darkness.

Chris

Smoke and Mirrors
June

The Beethoven Dance

When Lizey and I were much littler lasses, say nine and five, Dad instituted a Quiet Time policy after dinner. When we had finished eating and Mum (always Mum) had cleared the table, Lizey and I were sent over to the couch to "read, play and digest quietly." Television was "*streng verboten.*" We could do whatever we liked as long as we kept quiet and kept to the other side of the living room. Mum and Dad remained at the table. Dad would pour them each another glass of wine, light both their after-dinner cigarettes and put on some classical music. He and Mum would read or talk quietly while Lizey and I watched the clock. The music Dad chose then—and often still chooses now—was almost invariably booming, intense and cheerless. Particular selections of Beethoven, Liszt and Chopin were on high rotation. Occasionally he would put on some Sibelius, which was much less stressful and seemed to herald his being in a better mood. Mum preferred piano pieces to Dad's booming orchestral selections—she liked Granados, Rodrigo, Mompou. But these never seemed to feature in Quiet Time. She listened to them when she was cooking and cleaning in the kitchen. Alone.

Lizey was the more mischievous of the two of us, had a shorter attention span and was also a keen dancer. I was Easily Led. These factors combined to result in one of our favorite Quiet Time games—the Beethoven Dance. The Beethoven Dance had its genesis when Beethoven's Ninth Symphony was the favorite, although the game was by no means confined to Beethoven alone. The furious pace, earnestness and intensity of the second movement—and Dad's heartfelt enjoyment of it—begged for some mild mockery.

The Beethoven Dance was choreographed by Lizey and relied on both movement and facial expression, as noise of any kind was forbidden. In exaggerated fashion, we would march in circles in time with the music, our faces masks of maniacal concentration, turning with a flourish this way and that. As the music increased in pace and intensity, we would break the ranks of the marching circles and break into a gallop on imaginary horses. We'd gallop around the room in a figure eight, keeping in time with the music, of course, and occasionally encouraging the horses with imaginary riding crops.

Lizey made up little extra moves for us to alternate, matching the musical flourishes. When the final notes of the piece sounded, we fell "dead" to the floor, laughing hysterically but, as per QT requirements, silently. At least 80 percent of the Beethoven Dance's purpose was to raise a response from Dad. He usually feigned unawareness and studied his newspaper/script/New Yorker with great concentration and his specs perched low on his nose. But as the finale approached, a hint of a smile could sometimes be seen playing around the edges of his mouth and there would perhaps be a faint shake of his head.

"Girls," Mum would say, hiding her own smile in a sip of wine.

Tonight is Thursday and one of the two weeknights that I don't work. Dad is home for at least the next month. Jess has been in bed since seven. Mum, Dad and I have finished dinner. It's approaching eight-thirty. I push my chair back and adjourn to the couch. In our little house, the dining room is also the living room and the TV room. And of course the smoking room. Quiet Time having long since fallen by the wayside, I settle down to watch my favorite hospital drama.

"Amelia," says my father. "Can't we have some nice music instead?"

I glare at him. "If I could record the show and watch it later, after the smokers have retired for the evening, I would. But seeing as we don't have that capability, I have to watch it live."

Our VCR-DVD player packed it in over a year ago and a new one has not been purchased. He doesn't have a comeback for that but tells me to keep the sound down low. My back is turned to both of them as the opening credits conclude. I hear the hateful sound of him tapping a cigarette out of the pack, of Mum taking it, then of him tapping out another for himself. I brace for the click and flare of the cigarette lighter. When the acrid smoke wafts over to my nostrils, I sink my mouth and nose below my T-shirt collar. It doesn't help. I concentrate on hearing the dialogue on TV over Mum and Dad's voices.

At the first ad break I turn to give Dad one of my best glares. Glaring is the sole form of protest I dare to make about the smoke. As I wrote in my letter to Chris, Dad's anger is to be feared and me "whining" about the smoking is a surefire way to incur it.

The first time I ever stared down its barrel was seven years ago, when I was eight. I hung NO SMOKING signs all around the house, like I told Chris. Then I pilfered all the cigarettes and lighters in the house (including two cartons of stashed-away duty-free Winstons) and threw them into a Dumpster in the alley.

Come six, Dad was angry. Angry, craving nicotine and in no mood to find his crusading eight-year-old daughter cute. He does shout—but it's not the volume that is so terrifying. He somehow manages to strike a tone that decimates any opposition, that saps your ability to fight back. The verbal equivalent of that paralyzing goo those dinosaurs from *Jurassic Park* spit into the faces of their prey. Once you're immobilized, you know you are powerless, and that sucks. Strange too what makes him angry and what doesn't.

Last time Lizey was home, she borrowed the family car and backed it into a pillar in a parking garage. Hard. She drove straight home and in faltering tones told Dad what had happened. She was scared shitless about what he would say. He calmly inspected the scratched paintwork, the smashed taillights and the huge dent in the back panels.

Lizey burst into tears and blubbered apologies.

"Now, darling," he said, with a brief clap on her shoulder. "These things happen. You'll know to be extra careful in future."

And that was the end of the matter.

My glare during the commercial break doesn't manage to catch either Mum's or Dad's eye. My father exhales smoke as he talks about the playwright of the play he is directing at the Brooke Street Theatre.

"—he comes to almost every rehearsal and watches me like a hawk. Interrupts the actors if he thinks they've stressed the wrong word or failed to stress the word he intended. Doesn't seem to understand that once the play is written and printed, his job is done and mine begins."

"Oh dear," Mum murmurs, nodding slowly as she pulls in another lungful of smoke.

"In the third act, I'm trying to increase the pace as rapidly as possible, which is in large part achieved through the dialogue. If I follow every last comma he's put in there, it interferes with the pace. So I tell the actors that increasing the pace and the energy between them takes priority over following the punctuation and italics that this man has obsessively put in. Parts of his script seem to confound what I *think* he's trying to achieve. Anyway, he's up in arms about the dialogue being lost. The dialogue is everything! Well, of course it is to him, but I have to make the whole thing work on a stage."

"Of course you do," Mum says.

"Good dialogue is everything. *Effective* dialogue is everything. Not dialogue *per se.*"

"Quite right."

"After rehearsal last night I had a couple of drinks with the cast in the foyer. He's looking even more troubled than usual and he corners me and says, 'Look, Robert, I can't help but wonder, what do you really think of the script?' 'Well, Peter,' I replied, 'it *strains* for a crystallizing moment.'"

"Oh, *darling!*" Mum shakes her head, ashing her cigarette.

"Well, what a whiner! I'm being hounded by a twenty-six-year-old with a lot to learn about theater when I have a job to do. He's holding me back; he's putting the actors off, and we open in two weeks."

"Yes, but why put him off? Why be incendiary? Especially to a man who is touted to become the finest playwright of his generation."

"I don't care what he's touted as. He needs to let me do my job."

"Hmmmmm."

Mum's disapproval is perfunctory, kind of like Dad's disapproval of the Beethoven Dance. You can tell she likes that he won't suck up to anyone. Even though if he had been nicer to the right people over the years, he might have scored a cushy residency at a Sydney theater instead of having to travel all over the place, living production to production.

"Would you like another cigarette, darling?"

"Yes, thanks."

That's it. I stand up, punch the OFF button on the television and stalk out of the room. It was a crap episode anyway.

"Looks like Amelia got miffed and flounced out of the room," I hear Dad smirk to Mum. That's one of his favorite phrases. I give him plenty of opportunity to use it.

Upstairs in my little bedroom, I sit on my bed, leaning back against the thin plaster wall that separates my room from Jess's. My clothes and hair smell of smoke. I am still fuming. So to speak. It's interesting how fuming, or anger in general, is such a physical process, like a wave washing up on a beach and then receding.

There's wisdom in not pissing certain people off. It's plain that neither of my parents really subscribes to that theory. Further to this wisdom, I think, is that cozying up to the right people can get you places that "being yourself" will never get you.

Or being *myself* anyway. Take Coles, for example. The ruler of that particular roost is Bianca. She rules socially and also practically, because she is the most senior service supervisor. There is a core group of minions that surround her—Jeremy Horan, Street Cred Donna and a couple of others. They are all in my year or thereabouts. They all adhere to a certain code of flattery, submission, and smoke-break etiquette involving varying degrees of flirtation.

Being a supervisor, Bianca gets to decide who has to work on the registers and who gets to come off them during quiet times, ostensibly to collect trolleys and put away stray stock, but really to entertain her. Obviously, she favors her minions in this process and they get to spend a lot of time off the registers. They also get to spend a lot of time at Bianca's parental manor, putting a large dent in her father's wine cellar. Chris, Ed and Kathy are also "in," but they exist *alongside* Bianca, rather than below her, because they are a similar age.

I occupy a certain no-man's-land at Coles. I'm definitely not in with Bianca and her minions. I could argue that I'm of such pure spirit that I refuse to cozy up. Perhaps closer to the truth is that I just don't know *how* to. In truth, a part of me longs to be huddled with them out at the back loading dock to the exclusion of everyone else, smoking and laughing and then off to the pub after work. The only reason that I am not a complete reject at work is because of my friendship with Chris, which is, I suspect, completely mystifying for most people. They skate around me with wary smiles and take care not to be openly rude or dismissive, unsure of the amount of social capital I might be hoarding. Chris doesn't cozy up to anyone, as such. He just turns on his charm to full voltage and people like him because he makes them laugh and feel good. He's confident. Where did he get that? Can I get it?

I'm tired. Tomorrow is Friday. Basketball practice at 7:20 a.m. Double history, double math. Work after school from four till nine. I'll leave the house at 6:20 a.m. in my sports gear and take the bus(es) to school by 7:20. It's too cold to walk now that it's winter.

I pack my tote bag with my school sweater, white shirt, brown school shoes, skirt and tights. Then I pack my work uniform: black pants, black shoes, socks, red scarf and name badge. I battle to close the zipper, then test the bag's weight. Ouch.

I assemble and pack my school folders and textbooks in my backpack: chunky math book, gargantuan history folder, The Great War, calculator, French and English exercise books, French dictionary, Macbeth. I struggle to close that zipper too and end up having to take the history folder out. I'll have to put the school-bag on my back, the tote bag over one shoulder and carry the history folder in my arms. I must remember to put my bus pass in my track-pants pocket so I don't have to put everything down and fumble around in my backpack for my wallet when the bus comes.

I put my pj's on, clean my teeth, wash and moisturize my face. Then I pad into Jess's room to lean over her sleeping form and listen for her breathing. I reposition Prize Teddy next to her. They have never spent a night apart. I kiss her warm little cheek, inhale the delicious sleeping toddler aroma and pad out again.

Back in my room, I pause in front of the mirror long enough to ascertain that I look the same today as I did yesterday. In bed, I open my bedside table drawer, get out Chris's letter and run my eyes over his handwriting. I rub my feet together to warm them. Curling up in a ball, I think: Sun rises, sun sets, and still no Chris.

The Sisterhood

I don't know exactly how it happened, but some boys have been turning up where Penny and my group of friends sit at lunchtime. They bring their lunch. They sit and talk to us. Well, not to *me*, but to most of the others and always to Penny. The boys are all in our year. None of them are the rugby players I have mentioned before. My group would never qualify for a visit from them. I catch a few of their names. Daniel, Leonard, Sam, James. They are headed by a Scott that I don't like. I've seen him doing the rounds of other groups of girls this year. I reckon he fancies himself a bit of a player, something special for the ladies. Some of the boys need a hair wash, some deodorant and some Clearasil. They try very hard to appear relaxed. There is a lot of unconvincing laughter. Some of them nod to Penny as if they know her. She gives a flicker of recognition back.

"How do you know them?" I asked her in low tones the first day they came over.

"They catch my bus," she said, sitting straight-backed and unwrapping the sandwiches packed by her father.

Scott sits down on the other side of her and they talk for most of the lunch break.

I'm not quite sure how to conduct myself when Penny is otherwise occupied. I'm friends with the other girls in our group, but it's strange not to be part of my usual double act. Disconcerting. I talk to Eleni and Nicola—who are another tight twosome within the larger group—but my mind is not really on the conversation. By the end of the lunch period, there is a spark of anger in my chest that I try to push away.

I *have bigger fish to fry,* I tell myself.

When I arrive at work that afternoon, Chris is already on his register. Kathy is hovering near him, but I can see that the Kathy virus is in remission today, and hopefully for good.

I open my locker in the staff room to put away my backpack and tote bag. Inside is a folded-up piece of yellow paper that turns out to be several pages covered with Chris's blue script. I smile and stand still except for my thumb, which moves back and forth across the paper. I imagine holding Chris's hand—with fingers interlocking, not how your mother used to hold your hand—and moving my thumb across the join between his thumb and forefinger.

The staff room is suddenly filled with the chatter and shrill laughter of Alana and Kelly, who have also just arrived from school and smell of cigarettes.

"Hi," I say, but they don't hear me, or even seem to see me. I head out to the registers. *Bigger fish to fry,* I tell myself again.

"How the hell are you, Youngster?" Chris greets me warmly as I take the CLOSED sign down from the register next to his. "Did you get your little something?"

"Indeed I did. I'm looking forward to reading it."

"How was school today?"

"Well," I say. "There are boys sitting with us at lunchtime."

"How exciting!"

"Nah, it's not exciting. They're nothing special."

"Go easy on the fifteen-year-old boys, Youngster. They're doing the best they can."

"Well, I wish they'd do it somewhere else."

As if on cue, Jeremy Horan walks by on his way to the staff room, his gaze firmly averted from Chris and me. Actually, probably just from me.

"Hello, Jeremy!" Chris calls, with dangerously false heartiness.

There is nothing for Jeremy to do but look over and mutter, "Hey, Chris."

"And you remember Amelia, don't you?"

Jeremy glowers at Chris. "Yeah," he manages. "How's it going?"

"Exceedingly well, thank you, Jeremy." I beam and suppress a giggle.

"Off you go then, tiger," says Chris. "You'd better not be late to your register today—Bianca's not working."

Jeremy stalks off.

Chris smiles at me. "The way he carries on, it's as if your special moment never even happened."

"I know!" I fake incredulity. "Maybe . . . maybe it wasn't that special!"

"Now, that's just crazy talk."

I throw my hands up.

"Poor Jeremy, Alana and Kelly," says Chris as we watch the three of them slink back past us. "When Bianca's not here, they actually have to do some work."

"It's very, very sad."

"So sad. I wonder if Amnesty International is aware of it."

"How's your thesis going?" I change the subject.

"Oh, that old chestnut. I haven't really got a handle on it yet. But I have been conducting a very interesting experiment this week."

"Hypothesizing?"

"Hypothesizing that a twenty-one-year-old male can be indefinitely sustained on an intake of black coffee, red wine, organic dates and Tylenol."

"Hmm."

"It's already Wednesday and here I am, bright-eyed and bushy-tailed."

I study his face closely. The smudges under his eyes are darker than usual; his lips are dry and ashen, similar to the rest of his face. It's been a while between haircuts. Two days' worth of stubble. He's beautiful.

I hurry home when work finishes at nine, periodically checking that the letter is still in my pocket. The house is quiet. Dad is at rehearsal and Mum and Jess are in bed. There's a note from Mum informing me that my dinner is in the oven. I retrieve a foil-covered white bowl from the oven. As I remove the foil, a flurry of steam escapes and burns my wrist. I yelp and peer into the bowl. Noodle stir-fry with pork and vegetables. It smells great and I'm starving. Thank you, Mum. I sit down at the dining table with a fork in one hand and the letter in the other.

Greetings, Youngster!

Today I come to you from a lecture on the Bay of Pigs fiasco. At least, according to the course outline it is supposed to be a lecture on the Bay of Pigs fiasco. I actually have no idea what the lecturer is talking about, and I am amazed that any human being, let alone one who is supposedly a professional communicator, could achieve such a level of unintelligibility. If I'd known it was this guy lecturing, I'd have gone straight to the uni bar. But no, I came skipping into the lecture theater and took a seat in the middle of a center row. I can't get out without climbing over at least fifteen people and drawing all kinds of attention to myself. I'm stuck here for another forty-five minutes.

I was thinking about what you said that time we went for pizza, about how your mum is getting screwed by this, our modern age. From your (somewhat simplistic) vantage point, feminism has earned her the right to work full-time, do the housework, bear the children and look after them. I'm still not sure where feminism fits into it, but you are right about her getting screwed. I've read a lot of articles in the <u>Herald</u> about how workforce participation for women has grown steadily over the last thirty or so years but hasn't been accompanied by a rise in the share of domestic duties taken on by men. I believe it. My mum does most of the cooking and cleaning in our house. Always has. My dad feigns incompetence. At least, I assume he is feigning it.

Maybe it's a generational thing. Our mums got screwed because they're a generation who could get into the workplace, earn an independent wage and occupy their minds outside the domestic realm. It was only once they got there that they realized that full-time workers really need a wife to run the home and look after the children. But women don't get one! Hey, wait a minute! You mean I have to do it all? Yes, they have to. In fact, they are expected to work and earn money now, because the days of a household and a mortgage being sustained on one wage are OVER Red Rover.

Perhaps subsequent generations will change the pattern. But I don't think so, because we've all grown up watching our mothers "having it all," and hence doing it all, while our fathers watch TV and wait to be called down for dinner. When you grow up, Youngster, and shack up with some guy, he'll be used to not doing housework and you'll be used to the woman doing it, 'cause that's what you both grew up with. There'll be periodic fights about it, you'll say it's just not acceptable and that it won't do, and he'll nod solemnly and promise to make a change. For a few weeks after a fight you might come home to find the bed made, the dishes washed and your best glad rags ruined in a giant, indiscriminate, well-meaning load of laundry. But sometime in your mid-to-late twenties you'll realize that consistent, equal contribution to household duties is just not programmed into his system and you can either break up with him or put up with it. Who knows what you and the lasses of your generation will choose....

But when I started to write this letter, I wanted to tell you more about feminism. I was impressed that your teacher gave <u>The Feminine Mystique</u> to a class of fifteen-year-old girls. You said that Betty Friedan was part of what is known as second-wave feminism? Did you know that it was preceded by first-wave feminism (duh!) and followed by third-wave feminism? Has your crazy English teacher taken you there yet? All this you will learn when you come to university to go for a liberal arts degree like me. Allow me to give you a short tutorial. You must have seen <u>Mary Poppins</u> as a child. You may even have watched it over and over like my sister Zoe did, and, well, I was in the vicinity. From the children's father's first song (what a jerk!) we gather that the year is 1910. The mother sings her opening song as she is arriving home from a day of lobbying for women's suffrage, or the right to vote. She's wearing her suffragette's sash. She's singing about all the suffragettes casting off the shackles of yesterday and marching shoulder to shoulder with their sisters into the fray. Then there are cries of "Votes for women!" and talk of a fellow activist who has been arrested for her efforts. Generally speaking, these sorts of movements are thought of as first-wave feminism, or the first wave of "Fuck this!"

In the late nineteenth and early twentieth centuries, some women were writing and protesting about how they were second-class citizens. They didn't have the vote, they were widely discriminated against and they were essentially the property of men, especially in marriage. Then, in the 1960s, the second wave of "Fuck this!" began, where the floodgates of feminist scholarship were opened and there was prolific writing and lobbying for women's rights in education, the workplace, the legal system, the health system and, well, etcetera. Heaps and heaps of strands of feminism were born here, which you will learn all about when you come to university.

There are some especially interesting feminist analyses of marriage, which would be very

pertinent to your observations of your parents'
marriage. Even the liberal feminists see marriage
as a major tool for maintaining patriarchy.
Anyways, then third-wave feminism came along,
beginning in the 1980s, and pointed out quite
rightly that the "oppression of women" descried
by the first and second waves referred mainly
to middle-class and somewhat educated white
women. Who had every right to do so and made
many valid points, but they used the terms _women_
and _feminism_ as if they applied to every woman in
the world regardless of class and ethnicity.

   The thirdies are conscious of the differences
among women and the different "vectors of
oppression" and inequality across societies. What
we Western scholarly types had always called
feminism is actually _a_ feminism. Does your head in,
huh?

   My favorite writer is called Kate Jennings—
mention her to your wacky English teacher,
Youngster, I cannot recommend her to you enough.
She will tell you what you need to know about
life. She will not gild the lily or beat around the
bush. She will tell it to you like it is, and while
sobering you up completely, she will also make

you laugh. She belongs to no one and she's not afraid. Here is a taste of her take on second- and third-wave feminism:

> "Well-meaning waffle about sisterhood was replaced by more sophisticated but equally dubious pronouncements about "difference," in the sense of plurality. It is easy, of course, to give lip-service to pluralism—politicians are forever conjuring up rainbows and mosaics, while feminists favour braids and quilts—another matter altogether to accommodate it."

Aren't you excited about coming to university? You can sit around discussing this stuff all day—no math, no biology! Just don't take the History of American Foreign Policy. It may kill you.

Well, Youngster, I hope the above will come in handy for making you look smart in front of your English class, although I'm sure you do already. Here are my closing words on "difference" and "vectors of oppression," seeing as how the thirdies have got us thinking about it. In a lot of sociology classes that I have been to and in a lot of scholarship in general, people illustrate "difference" by contrasting us folks from prosperous, "lucky" backgrounds with people from developing or war-torn countries. A blind man can see that there are huge differences between the prospects and experiences of people like us vs. people who live in daily fear of militiamen coming to bulldoze their homes, rape the women and children and then shoot everyone in the head. That's too easy a contrast. You know what, Youngster? We don't need to look nearly as far away. I'll bet that when you think of Sydney, you think of the terrain of your life here. The suburbs where you and your mates live, your route to school and to work, the beaches where you go to swim in the summer, the city where you might go for shopping or movies and wherever else is on high rotation in your life. I bet you don't think of the public housing ghettos in, say, Morton, with twenty-year-old mothers of three who have no idea about a life that doesn't involve violence and welfare-dependent poverty. I bet you're even saying, "Where the hell is Morton?" It's a suburb between Mount Druitt and St. Marys, out west. There's no train line or state transit buses, and a lot of private bus companies won't operate there. Want to really do your head in? Spend a morning at the Morton drop-in center and then the afternoon at Kirribilli Yacht Club.

You don't have to look very far to see difference, Youngster. Don't think it's safely far away.

Thank God. This guy is wrapping it up at last.

Harvey out

Overstimulated, I lean back in my chair for a few minutes. Then I take my empty bowl to the kitchen, rinse it and put it in the dishwasher. It's almost ten. Homework time—although I'd love to read the letter again and again. I carry my backpack upstairs. It's dark except for the glow of Jess's night-light. In my room I switch on my desk lamp and unpack my books. The letter goes in my top drawer with the other one.

It's midnight when I get to bed. As I'm drifting off, I hear Dad arriving home from rehearsal.

Maturity

It's seven o'clock. I am showered, dressed in my school uniform and in Jess's bedroom beginning the process of getting her up.

"Come on!" I clap my hands. "Let's get this show on the road!"

She frowns without opening her eyes, makes non-compliant sounds and tightens her grip on Prize Teddy.

I open the curtains so the sun streams onto her face. "Jess, you're going to make Mum stressed and late for work. We don't want that."

No response.

"I'm gonna pull the covers off in a minute!"

"Nooooooo."

I look at my watch. I don't have time for this. I have to get Jess dressed now so I can have Mum's tea and toast ready by the time she comes downstairs. I go to the foot of the bed, grab hold of the covers and pull them off in one swift movement.

Jess makes more non-compliant noises.

I pull her up into a sitting position. She makes herself a deadweight. I turn to ferret her preschool clothes out of the chest of drawers. When I turn around, she has collapsed back onto the bed.

I grab hold of her arm quite roughly and hiss, "Jess, you're getting up NOW! Right now or Teddy is going to hang out the window!"

That does the trick. She stands up on the bed and lifts her arms over her head for me to remove her pajama top. I feel bad, but what else could I do? Anyways, that's lightweight stuff compared to some of the stunts that Liza used to pull on me. Like convincing me that on my sixth birthday Mum and Dad were going to give me to an orphanage.

I help Jess with her tracksuit and socks. Her sneakers have Velcro straps (very exciting), so I leave her to put them on herself. Mum is blow-drying her hair in the bathroom as I go downstairs.

I am first into the kitchen. I pull open the venetian blinds and the sun streams in, highlighting the dust that has just been knocked off the wooden slats. I put the kettle on and place two slices of soy and linseed bread in the toaster. I get out a cup, a tea bag, a plate, a knife, the sugar bowl, peanut butter, jam and milk. I spread peanut butter on one slice of toast and jam on the other. Savory first, I think, then sweet. Mum likes her tea strong, with a splash of milk and between a quarter and half a teaspoon of sugar. Not everyone can pull it off.

I hear Mum and Jess fighting on the way down the stairs.

"I want to watch TV!" Jess is whining.

"No. No TV in the morning."

"Yes! Watch TV!"

"No. I said no."

Jess's high-pitched yell gets louder and louder until it ceases and I hear the Sesame Street music wafting down the hall.

Mum appears in the kitchen, defeated. She bangs a few things around in the sink, then sits down to her tea and toast.

"I'll be home a bit late this afternoon," she says. "Staff meeting after school."

One of Mum's colleagues—and her closest friend at work—was threatened by a student with a knife earlier in the week. I'd come home to find Mum smoking in the backyard at four. She only ever does that when something horrible has happened at school. For years there's been talk of Riley Street High being closed down because there are so many problems with it. Whenever an incident happens—like the massive brawl with Enmore High at a basketball match—the politicians go on TV and say, "Riley Street High School is a blight on the face of Sydney and it should be bulldozed!"

They love that word, bulldozed. They reckon a lot of things should be bulldozed. Aboriginal housing projects. Youth drop-in centers. Safe injecting rooms. Lots of public high schools.

It's as clear this morning as it is every other morning that my carefully considered savory-then-sweet toast selection and my painstakingly concocted cup of tea have not had the desired effect. That is, they have not in any way shifted the despair from Mum's existence. *It wouldn't matter what I made her for breakfast. I could serve up blueberry and ricotta pancakes with freshly brewed coffee and she'd still be miserable.* I hover about the kitchen helplessly.

"Do you want me to put Jess's milk on?" I venture.

Jess refuses to eat breakfast—she will, however, accept a cup of hot Ovaltine. The milk has to be warmed in a saucepan on the stove. I have suggested the purchase of a microwave oven to warm up the milk in twenty seconds, among other uses, but this seems to provoke arguments with and between my parents.

"No, I'll do it," Mum replies. She stands up and bangs the saucepan down on the burner. Mum's despair usually swings between two ends of a spectrum—Sad and Wordlessly Shitty. This morning it's definitely swinging toward Wordlessly Shitty. There's nothing for me to do but go to school. So I go.

After dinner that evening, I take the phone into my room, place it in front of me on the bed and regard it for several minutes. I've never rung Chris at home, never had the nerve. But I have to talk to him tonight. I count to three and dial the number.

Blood is thudding in my ears and all the muscles in my abdomen twist uncomfortably.

"Hello?" answers a young woman.

"Hi! Ah, could I please speak to Chris, please." One *please* would have been enough.

"Certainly. Who's calling?"

"Amelia Hayes."

"Just a moment."

There's some scrabbling around and I hear her saying, "Chris, it's for you. Amelia Hayes."

I think there's some mockery in the way she said my name. *Why the hell didn't I just say Amelia? Think Street Cred Donna. Imagine you've got a stud through your bottom lip and a tattoo on your bicep.*

"Good evening, Youngster." Chris's blessed tones.

"Hi, Chris. What . . . what are you up to?"

"My sister and I are watching Media Watch."

"Oh . . . should I call back?"

"Nah, it's almost finished. What's up?"

"Well, I was wondering, I . . . needed to run something by you . . . 'cause I don't get it. . . ."

"What's up, Youngster?" It's his Patient Tone. He often adopts the Patient Tone when talking to me.

Here goes . . .

"What the HELL is up with the ending of Great Expectations?"

Backing up a tiny bit, at lunch that day I'd been sitting with Penny in our usual spot. The lunch period goes from 12:40 to 1:20. Right on cue at 12:55, the boys that have been blessing us with their company of late come ambling across the grass. They are led by that dreadful Scott, who is way more pleased with himself than he has reason to be. He's taken to parking himself next to Penny, reclining with legs outstretched, propping himself up on one elbow like Caecilius, the Pompeii dude from our seventh-grade *Ancient Rome* textbook, and regaling her with his wit. He never, ever acknowledges me, even though I'm always sitting next to Penny when he levers himself in. I keep expecting Penny to tell him he's a tool and to get lost, but she doesn't. So, lately, I've taken to reading at lunchtime. Surrounded by the forced laughter and novice flirtation of my peers, I bury my head in a book, signaling to all that I strongly disapprove. I wonder if anyone even notices.

Today I read the last five pages of *Great Expectations*. And I need to talk to Chris.

"Uh-oh," says Chris.

"What the hell!"

"Now steady on—"

"*I saw no shadow of another parting from her!* What does that mean? It can't mean that they're going to get together. Tell me that's not what it means."

"That's what it means."

"Then what was the point of any of it? What's the lesson that Pip learns, that *we* learn from him?"

"Well—"

"For 493 pages I put up with Pip's shit, put up with him being cruel to the people who loved him and continuing to run around after those who didn't. Put up with all the ridiculous 'smoke and mirrors,' the illusions, the false conclusions, the 'Ooh, So-and-so is really So-and-so's father; So-and-so is really Miss Havisham's jilting fiancé; So-and-so was Pip's true benefactor; So-and-so was actually the one who made Mrs. Gargery into a vegetable.' I put up with it all in the hope that at the end the bullshit would be debunked and the characters would see things as they are. Pip would finally see Estella and Miss Havisham for the cruel bitches they were. He would learn to accept his defeat gracefully, and—unlike Gatsby—get on with his life."

"We don't always get what we want, do we? Especially with, you know, wanting other people. But it's worth something to finally see clearly, isn't it?"

"Well, I think so."

"Then what was Dickens thinking? What was the point of the whole series of events if not for the hero to mature?"

"Well—"

"*I saw no shadow of another parting from her! What he should have said was: I see plenty of shadows of another parting from her, because I choose it to be so. I have lingered long enough in this great ruined place, emotionally and physically, and it's time for me to move on.*"

"Maybe Dickens was worried that his readers would revolt if they didn't get a happy ending for Pip and Estella," Chris offers, finally getting a sentence in edgewise.

"Then he should have had more respect for his readers," I splutter. "If I want a happy ending I'll watch Pretty Woman. Bloody Pip! He should have married Biddy when he had the chance, gotten a job and shut up. Sure, we all want Estella, but we don't always get what we want, do we?"

"No," says Chris, with a hint of Gutted Tone. "We do not."

"I had great expectations. Of that book."

"Do you know that Dickens originally wrote a different ending for the book? One where they don't get together?"

"No way."

"Yes way. Pip and Estella go their separate ways. Pip goes off to work in various places. Estella gets beaten to a pulp by her brute of a husband, who eventually gets killed by a horse he is mistreating. Then she marries the doctor who looked after her after one of the beatings. Pip and Estella run into each other in the street some years later and exchange civilities. Pip is satisfied that she has seen enough suffering to understand what he went through for all those years, but what he really means is that he's satisfied that she's had her comeuppance."

"That's a much better ending. What happened to that one?"

"He got persuaded out of it by Edward Bulwer-Lytton."

"Who is Edward Bulwer-Lytton?"

"He's the genius that originally came up with *It was a dark and stormy night*."

"No!"

"Yes."

"That's depressing."

"Yeah." I hear him stretch and yawn. "So you had your heart set on Pip growing up, huh?"

"I wanted him to get his comeuppance. To realize he's let himself be had all these years."

"But he never got over his fear of Virginia Woolf."

"He what?"

"Never mind. It's from—well, I won't tell you what it's from. You'll stumble upon it one day and think, Ah! *That's what Chris meant when he said . . .*"

Brief silence. I get my breath back. I wish Chris would come and live with me in my little bedroom.

"Well, Youngster, I must go. Try sticking to twentieth-century texts. Lots of confronting reality there."

"See you at work."

"Ah." He yawns again. "Yes."

I hang up and ponder on my bed for a few minutes. Then I

get to my feet and descend the stairs, clutching my copy of *Great Expectations*. I pause in the downstairs hallway, craning my head toward the back steps leading down to Dad's study. Sibelius's Fifth Symphony wafts from underneath the closed study door. I am heartened—Sibelius's Fifth means he's in a good mood. It could make the stoniest of hearts tremble.

I knock softly on the door.

"Come in."

And I do. He's sitting in the big chair by the window, cigarette in one hand, a copy of the *Spectator* in the other. I turn the volume down a touch.

"Dad."

"Yes, darling." He ashes the cigarette with a delicate forefinger.

"What does it mean to be afraid of Virginia Woolf?"

He frowns. "What?"

I wave my copy of G.E. in the air.

"If I said, 'Well, clearly Pip is afraid of Virginia Woolf,' what does that mean?"

He smiles. Then he puts his cigarette to rest on the ashtray, lays the *Spectator* on the arm of the chair, stands up and scans one of his bookshelves. He takes down a slim paperback, browned with age, and hands it to me. *Who's Afraid of Virginia Woolf?* by Edward Albee.

"Read it and see," he says, returning to his chair.

Bathurst

For the first time in ages I am not working on the weekend. I'm going to Bathurst on the train to visit Lizey. I've wanted to go all year but have been too afraid to ask Bianca, who does the roster, if I could have a weekend off. When I told Chris, he frog-marched me down to the service desk and stood beside me as I asked Bianca. She said yes.

Behind her, Jeremy was sitting on the glass counter, all boredom and carefully contrived sangfroid. His red bow tie was missing and his name badge askew. I was directly in his line of vision, but he managed to look right past me. I thought how funny it would be if the glass counter he was sitting on should break. Then he might have to have a facial expression.

"When do you leave, Youngster?" Chris asks as we walk toward the staff exit at the end of the night.

"Tomorrow morning. I catch the early train from Central."

"Well, you be careful of those uni students. I wouldn't trust most of 'em with a pretty fifteen-year-old girl."

Pretty! Me, pretty! Wait—he does mean me, right? Or is he just making a general statement?

"Yes, you," he says, reading my mind.

I smile down at the steps. We walk outside and down the street toward Chris's bus stop, where I'll leave him and continue my walk home alone.

There is silence. My head fills with the sound of a strange, overpowering "inner Amelia" screaming, I LOVE YOU! I LOVE YOU!

"Hey, Chris," I say, in an effort to drown it out.

"Yes, tiger?"

"Martha is afraid of Virginia Woolf."

"Wow, that didn't take you long. Very impressive."

"And probably most people are."

"Probably."

"You are."

"I what?"

We stop walking and face each other. I continue bravely, "Well, you won't give up the ghost. At least in the end George and Martha give up their ghost."

"What ghost?"

Careful. Careful.

"Well, how long have you clung to the Kathy ghost? Any fool could see that she ain't all that."

"What have you got against Kathy?" he asks, raising one eyebrow.

"Nothing!" I say hastily. "Nothing. Just, you know, she isn't nice to you, is she?"

"No."

"Neither was that Michaela chick." *Daring, Amelia, very daring!* He gives me a sharp look, and I quickly change the subject.

"Did Kathy find out, you know, about the poem and flowers?"

"Don't know. Don't care."

"It was a great poem."

"It was a *terrible* poem. But I was counting on her not catching on to that. I doubt that textual analysis is her strong suit."

"Oh."

We've reached the bus stop.

"I knew you'd like Virginia Woolf," he says.

"Yeah . . . well, yeah. I'll see you later then."

"Right. Safe traveling. Lay off the white wine."

"Will do." I turn to cross the street, and then turn back. "Hey, Chris?"

"Qué?"

"There *are* girls who would be really, really nice to you. If you'd, you know, pick them."

"Are there? Where?" He makes a show of looking up and down the street and underneath the seats in the bus shelter.

Say it! hollers inner Amelia. *Say, "One is standing right in front of you."*

I shrug. Not superbly. And I turn and walk home.

On Saturday, I wake at five to get the bus in to Central. Everyone is asleep when I leave the house toting my Billabong backpack and sporting my Nanna-knitted gray beanie. It's a chilly morning. I buy a cappuccino, a chocolate iced doughnut, an egg and lettuce sandwich and a bottle of water. I've brought a book to read—*The Robber Bride* by Margaret Atwood—but I spend the first hour of the journey looking out the window.

The train winds its way through Sydney heading west toward the Blue Mountains. We pass through Strathfield, Auburn, Granville, Parramatta, Westmead.

At Blacktown, a girl gets on the train with a toddler. She looks only a bit older than me. Her hair is greasy, her skin covered in acne, she wears dirty polyester track pants and there is a bruise on her left cheekbone. Her eyes are hard. The toddler sets up a shrill whine and thrashes around in his seat.

"Shut the fuck up, Cody!" the girl snarls. She fishes a large bag of chips out of her bag, opens them and gives them to the toddler. He sits quietly and eats them.

As the train pulls out of Mount Druitt, we run parallel to a main road for a few hundred yards. I see a large sign pointing to a turnoff: Morton. Morton! I hear Chris's voice saying, *You don't have to look very far to see difference.*

The toddler is whining again. His mum gets out a bottle of Coke and gives him a few sips. They get off the train somewhere called Emu Plains.

For the rest of the journey I read my book and have conversations with Chris inside my head. These conversations have become a favorite, and pretty much compulsive, pastime. In them, I am always witty, sometimes even sassy. In them, I have complete control.

The train pulls into Bathurst Station at about eleven. The sky is low and gray. Even through the glass, I can feel that it's much colder than Sydney. I leap out onto the platform and see Lizey down at the other end. There's a cute-ish guy with her.

We hurry toward each other and hug tightly, mumbling "Hey" into each other's hair. It's so good to see her and have her within my grasp. I don't want the hug to end yet, but she breaks away.

She looks essentially the same, but I scan for minute changes. Since moving away she's gained an almost mythical status at home, especially with Jess. Jess goes crazy with delight when Lizey makes her flying visits. She pulls out all her toys, brings all her little friends in from the street to soak up the glory of the returning big sister, wants only Lizey to push her on the swing and watch her go down the slide. They bake biscuits together in the kitchen. She asks after Lizey all the time—often when we're doing some quality-time activity like reading her favorite Spot books.

"'Naughty Spot. It's dinnertime—'"

"Is Lizey coming over this weekend?"

Why would Lizey be coming over this weekend?

"No. 'Where could he be? Is he out in the flower bed?'"

"When is she coming over?"

"I don't know, Jess. But I'm here, okay? I'm here."

And so forth.

"This is my housemate Jonno," says Lizey, turning to the guy who's loped up behind her. "He's got a car, so we won't have to walk."

Jonno tips an imaginary hat with the top of an imaginary walking cane.

"How come you're both wearing the same outfit?" I ask as we walk out into the car park. They're both in jeans, Converse shoes and checked flannel shirts.

"Oh," says Lizey, laughing, "Big W had a sale on flannels. Nothing like a flannel to keep out the Bathurst chill."

"That's right, ma'am," Jonno says.

We pile into Jonno's early-eighties-model Subaru two-door hatch.

While we're driving, Lizey tells me that they're having a party at their place tonight. I'd envisioned having her to myself so I could debrief at length about our parents and tell her about Chris. Lizey is good with boys. She's almost never without one. But a party could be good too. It will be good practice for Chris's world.

The ancient Subaru pulls up in front of a row of dilapidated terraces.

"This is us." Lizey bounds out and puts her seat forward. I struggle out with my backpack.

It turns out that the whole block is student housing. Lizey takes me out back first and I see that there are no fences dividing the backyards. It's just one big expanse of overgrown grass, dotted with clusters of upturned milk crates, collapsed clotheslines and a couple of scuzzy-looking barbecues.

"One big family." She grins, gesturing to a few people lounging on neighboring back steps, nursing coffee cups or with cigarettes dangling from their fingers.

We head back inside to meet the other housemates, Guy and Lucy, who are sitting at the kitchen table. They are both in pajamas and bathrobes. Empty toast plates and mugs are in front of them. They smoke languorously, ashing their cigarettes into a round biscuit tin. Then we go upstairs to Lizey's bedroom.

She's never been tidy like me. The bed is unmade, clothes are strewn everywhere and one of her old sarongs is serving as a curtain.

I put my backpack down and shiver. "It's freezing in here."

"It sure is," agrees Lizey. "I'll lend you a flannel shirt and a thermal."

"Hey, is that Jonno guy your boyfriend?"

"Jonno? Nah. He kind of was for a while but ... nah."

"Oh."

"I've actually got my eye on a boy from two doors up. Hoping to make some headway tonight."

We sit on her unmade bed. It has the same smell as her bed at home did. Essence of Lizey. Maybe that's a weird thing to notice. I like the smell. It means my sister is close by.

"So how are the parents?" she asks.

"Same old. Mum's miserable most of the time. Jess is cute. Dad is . . . Dad."

Lizey's flamboyance always seemed to lighten things up at home—even made Mum smile sometimes. Since she's been gone, there's been little or no comic relief. God knows there's none coming from me.

"I think his show at Brooke Street is going well."

Lizey remains quiet.

"Hey, I kissed a boy," I volunteer.

"You what?"

"I kissed a boy."

"When?"

"Few months ago."

"Where?"

"At a party."

"Well, good for you! Who was the lucky guy?"

"Uh, just some guy from work."

"Some Guy from Work. That's beautiful, that is. And has anything come of it?"

"Nah. He hasn't spoken to me since."

"Tool."

"Yeah."

"Want me to see if I can hook something up for you tonight?" she teases.

"Nooooowah!" I lie back on the pillows.

"So with the party tonight . . ."

"Yeah?"

"I'll look after you as much as I can, but if the chance presents itself for me to have some quality time with Ben, you might have to look after yourself."

"Who's Ben?"

"The boy from two doors up."

"Oh."

"You'll definitely be sleeping in here, but don't get freaked out if I don't end up here."

"Oh."

I must look a bit deflated because Lizey pokes me on the arm.

"Come on, you're a big girl now."

I prickle. *A big girl who got up in the pitch-black this morning and sat on a train for four and a half hours to spend some time with you,* I think mutinously. *So sue me if I don't want to spend a night alone in a strange, freezing-cold house with people I don't know!* I hate it when she makes those comments—they are the adult version of her childhood taunt "Don't be such a baby."

She looks out of her bedroom window from underneath the sarong, scanning the backyard below.

"Let's go and have a cup of tea in the garden," she says abruptly.

"It's cold out there," I protest, but she is already halfway to the door.

There's one bathroom in the house and you have to go out the back door to get to it. After sampling the temperature in there and inspecting the shower recess, I've decided to wait until I get home tomorrow night to have a shower. It's about six and I'm sitting on the bed watching Lizey put makeup on in front of her mirror. A sudden, aggressive loneliness takes hold of me. I'm nervous. I don't know anyone coming to this party. It will probably go for hours. I want Lizey. I want my mother.

"I miss you," I say, and start to cry.

Lizey turns around.

She re-caps the mascara wand she's holding and sits down beside me.

"What's up? What?"

But I don't even know. "I just feel sad," I manage, and sob a few times.

"Why?" she says. "Why?"

"I don't know. Everything. I wish you'd come home; I miss you. And I don't want you to leave me tonight, 'cause I don't know anyone here. And I wanted to talk to you tonight, not go to a party."

"Parties are *fun*, Amelia. I wanted you to have fun here." She shakes her head at me. "What did you want to talk to me about?"

My sobs have receded to mild sniffling and slightly labored breathing.

"Nothing," I say.

"Nothing?" she repeats.

She returns to the mirror and uncaps the mascara. "When your face dries off, I'll put some of this on you."

The night passes more or less uneventfully. The party mainly takes place in the communal backyard, although it's bloody freezing. I borrow one of Lizey's "dress" beanies. There are loud conversations going on all around about people and events I have no idea of. Some of Lizey's friends chat to me a little. Dinner is bread and dip. Most people are drinking beer, but I fill a large plastic cup from a four-liter box of red wine set up on one of the upturned milk crates. By the time I have drunk half of it, I feel decidedly less lonely.

Lizey points the Ben boy out to me. He is wearing a soft-looking denim jacket, a gray woolen scarf and a beanie that's more of a very large skullcap. He is very good-looking, and he knows it. I tend to be quite turned off by people who know that they are good-looking: like that dreadful Scott who's been sitting with us at school, like Kathy. I think they're best avoided. I'm lucky I will never be in the thrall of one of them. Although, I think, conjuring up the warmth of Chris's presence, I've not escaped a different kind of thrall.

I last until about ten, by which time I have consumed one and a half glasses of the boxed wine. I find Lizey in a small group of Ben and two other girls.

"I'm going to bed."

"Yeah?" She puts an arm around me.

"Yeah. See you"—I glance at Ben—"whenever. . . ."

I clean my teeth in the freezing bathroom with even-more-freezing water. The red wine has stained my tongue a grotesque shade of purple. I scrub at it with my toothbrush and spit out great gobs of purple toothpaste foam.

Lizey's bedroom is so cold that I almost can't bear to remove my body-warmed clothing and put on my icy pajamas. I'm tired and very fuzzy from the wine. I pull off my clothing as quickly as possible, suck in my breath, yank on my pj's, snap off the light and dive under the covers.

Lying alone in the big bed and looking at the dark ceiling, a pang of hunger for Chris twists my insides.

"Chris!" I say loudly, as if he could hear me. And I cry again, allowing myself a much freer rein this time, as there is no one about and no one can hear me. A wet patch collects on my pillow. I swap it for the other pillow. I think I sleep.

My train gets in to Central at about six on Sunday. I am stiff, dirty and fantasizing about a hot shower. Mum and Jess wait for me on the platform, holding hands. Mum wears her big dark overcoat, Jess her little blue parka with the fake-fur edging. Jess jumps up and down and then runs toward me. I scoop her up into my arms.

"Nanna sent a special scarf for Teddy!" she says.

"Excellent!" I kiss both of her spongy little cheeks and plonk her back down.

"Hi, Mum."

"Hi, darling," says Mum. And, uncharacteristically, we hug. It feels damn good.

Fraying Ropes

When I walk into the Land of Dreams on Tuesday afternoon, Chris is standing at the service desk, studying the roster and fastening his bow tie. My body immediately alters course, and I am at his side.

"Hello there," I say. And I smile at him, not unlike how Maria smiles at Captain von Trapp in the gazebo.

"Miss Hayes," he says, emphasizing each word without varying his intonation. The Land of Dreams seems to quieten behind us. "It's good to see you."

Chris is king of winning smiles and witty banter, but thus far there has been neither. There is a smile from him, though—less brilliant than usual but more genuine. It nourishes me.

A voice breaks through from somewhere above.

"Are we going to our registers or are we standing around chatting?"

Bianca. Always there to spoil a moment. I notice on the roster that she has put Chris on register two, near her at the service desk, and me way up the other end on register sixteen.

The shift drags without Chris on a nearby register to chat to. Between customers I gaze down the other end and watch Chris talking to Bianca and Ed.

Four till nine is a five-hour shift. A school day is six and a half hours. So the shifts are like another school day, minus lunch or recess, after an actual school day. At ten to nine, I see Ed and Chris conferring and looking at me. Then Ed walks up to register sixteen.

"Hello, Amelia," he says, quite formally.

"Hello, Ed," I say, following suit.

"I'm, uh, having a birthday party on Sunday next week." He fishes a slip of paper out of his pocket and gives it to me. "My parents are away. The plan is to head on back to my place straight from work on Sunday."

Chris can be seen holding up both his thumbs at me from register two.

"Excellent. Thank you. I'll be there. How old?"

"Nineteen," he says. "I better go cash up." And he's gone.

"Sunday next week," I tell Penny in math the next day.

"Isn't that the night before the history exam?" she says.

"Yeah, I think so. Hey, what do you think I should wear?"

"Amelia, we both know what you are going to wear."

Earlier in the year, Lizey had lent me a skirt and top to wear to a friend's sixteenth birthday party. Penny and I had gotten ready together at my place. At the last minute I changed back into my jeans and T-shirt and could not be dissuaded.

The next bell will signal lunchtime. Lunch used to mean forty minutes of chatting with Penny. It now means thirty minutes of the Scott show, which plays a daily matinee to a willing audience consisting of my best friend. I decide to bring it up with Penny. Gently, though, 'cause she doesn't respond well to out-and-out confrontation.

"Why do you talk to that jerk Scott every day?"

Whoops. Couldn't help myself.

She raises an eyebrow. That's never a good sign.

"He's a tool," I continue. "He sits there day after day thinking, I am so the Man. And instead of telling him to piss off, you encourage him! Then he just loves himself even more."

"You've given this a lot of thought," observes Penny, looking away.

"Well, yeah. And he's so rude. Every day he comes to sit with you, and he has never, not once, said hello to me. None of them have."

"Well, gee, Amelia." She looks at me now. "Do you think that could have anything to do with the death stares you sit there and give out? Your eyes could kill a man at ten paces."

"They're not men."

"You make it obvious that you think they're totally beneath you; you sit there on your high horse sending filthy looks or you bury your head in a book. Why would they say anything to you?"

"They're jerks."

"For God's sake, they're not that bad! And in case you haven't noticed, for some of us they're all that's going. We don't all measure boys against the Chris benchmark. No one else has a Chris. And I guarantee that if you weren't so bent on comparing every boy in the world to your idol, you might relax about Scott and his friends."

I sulk. "You don't like him, do you?"

But Penny declines to answer, making a show of continuing with her algebra. I glare down at mine and then out the window.

"I'll be home late from work on Sunday," I say to Mum.

It's about five and I am just home from Friday basketball practice. Mum sits at the kitchen table, sipping a cup of tea and listening to Classic FM. Two large, dirty frying pans are sitting on the sink. They are from last night's dinner and Dad was supposed to wash them up. I glance at them nervously.

"Oh?" she says.

"Bit of a birthday party for a guy from work."

"The one who gave you the flowers?"

"What? No, someone else."

"Right." She sips her tea.

"Don't you want to know where it is and what time I'll be back?"

"Well—"

"You don't care, do you? Where I go and what I do. I could be out doing drugs and having unprotected sex. I could be *dealing* drugs. I could be getting tattoos. I could be failing school. And you wouldn't even know." I'm not quite sure where this is coming from or why. I never go off at Mum. I'm too scared of upsetting her. Further. But I seem to have her attention now.

"Well," she says, "you could be doing all those things. But I don't think you are."

"Why? Why don't you think that? I could so be doing them!"

"Because I know you are a sensible girl."

No, I think, *because you know I'm a loser with no social skills and no life, so what possible trouble could I get into?* I stomp upstairs to my room.

My crankiness hasn't abated an hour later. I sit in my room glowering at the ceiling. I *know what this is about*, I think. I'm cranky 'cause I'm uncomfortably thirsty for Chris all the bloody time. The heart-twinging excitement of yestermonth is gone. Now it just grates. There is no relief. There is nothing to be done. There is no sign of a parachute. I think of Penny's comment from math: "Not everyone has a Chris."

I don't have a Chris! I think savagely.

"Amelia!" I hear my mother calling from the kitchen below.

"What?" I snap back, louder than necessary, but raising my voice feels good.

"Can you run Jess's bath?"

Opening Night

On Friday night I've been lined up to babysit Jess. Mum and Dad are going to the opening night of Dad's play at Brooke Street Theatre. Mum arrives home from work at the usual time, clutching shopping bags, Jess and Jess's little backpack, and looking very tired. She bangs various pots and pans as she puts away the shopping.

"Here, I'll do that," I say lamely. "You sit down."

She ignores me. I wonder whether to offer to make her a cup of tea, but in this kind of mood she'll probably say no. When she's finished putting away the shopping, she fills the kettle and gets down a mug and tea bag.

"You go and sit down," I say. "I'll bring it to you."

I give her some gentle shoves and finally succeed in getting her to flop down on the couch in the next room, where Jess is watching TV.

"I mightn't be able to get back up again," she mutters.

I bring her the tea. She takes a few sips, then places the mug on the coffee table. Within a minute she's dozed off.

I make some toast and honey for Jess and me. Mum wakes half an hour later, groggy and disoriented. She looks at her watch, hauls herself up and staggers upstairs. The shower is running a minute later, followed by the muffled sounds of the hair dryer.

"I wish Mummy didn't have to go out," says Jess, not looking away from the TV. "Mummy's tired."

I climb the stairs to the bathroom. The door is ajar and Mum is in there putting on makeup. I enter and sit on the side of the bath.

"Why do you have to go out tonight?" I say mutinously. "You need to rest. You've been working all week."

"Hmmmm," says Mum, concentrating on applying eyeliner.

"Why don't you just tell him you're not going? Tell him you don't have to go if you don't want to."

"Not go? What do you mean?"

"You shouldn't have to go out at the end of the week. You're so tired."

"I don't *have* to go. But it's Dad's opening night. Of course I'm going."

"But you're tired—"

"Don't worry about it; I'm *all right.*"

She bangs the cabinet door shut.

Dad appears at the bathroom door. He's wearing the Ralph Lauren navy shirt and aftershave we gave him for his birthday.

"Everything under control in here?"

I look down at the tiles, wondering how much of the conversation he heard.

"Mm-hmm," says Mum.

"Ready to leave in fifteen minutes, darling?"

"Yep."

"Bye, girls!"

Mum is wearing a brown crushed-satin skirt and matching top. Her necklace is the one made from metallic triangles that fan out across her collarbone. Liza has been trying to lift that necklace for years, but Mum won't part with it. She's a looker, my mother. No doubt about it.

The front door closes behind them. Jess is tearful for a minute but is easily cheered up by the prospect of a bubble bath and a ham and cheese mini-pizza that happens to be her older sister's specialty. I let her stay up way past her bedtime because I am lonely.

Slammer

On the morning of Ed's party I study halfheartedly for the history test, telling myself that I will also study when I get home. At midday, I shower and get into my work uniform. I pack clothes for the party: my darker jeans, the battered old Blundstone boots that Mum bought for me in the winter of eighth grade, my gray long-sleeved T-shirt and a light blue short-sleeved T-shirt to go over it. I also pack one of my only necklaces: a largish jade carving on a black velvet ribbon. I sneak into Mum's room and pocket her bottle of Coco.

The quiet, genuine Chris of the last few shifts is gone today. In fact, there is an almost manic quality to him.

"Youngster!" he yells when I walk past, giving a curt salute. He packs groceries more vigorously than usual. When Bianca takes him off register to collect trolleys, he crashes them into each other and bangs them into the impulse confectionery stands the whole way down to the trolley bay.

"Are you all right?" I ask him.

"All right? All right? I'm fucking fantastic!" he blusters.

Right.

We close up shop at six. Street Cred Donna heads straight outside for a smoke. The way she wears her work uniform, it easily translates into a going-out outfit—rolled-up sleeves, silver pendants dangling on leather straps, three earrings in each ear, dyed blond hair in a high ponytail with strands coming down on either side, short black skirt, laddered stockings, and boots that come up to just below her knees.

I get changed in the women's toilets and spray a minute

amount of Coco on my neck. I brush my hair in the mirror next to the loud and jostling Alana and Kelly. Bianca leans against the wall behind us, surveying her minions.

"Nice necklace," she says, pointing at my jade carving.

I am so surprised that I don't say anything right away. Alana and Kelly fall silent.

"Thanks," I manage.

"Yeah, it's great," Alana rushes to concur.

"So original," agrees Kelly.

I nod, and brush my hair furiously.

Bianca approaches the mirror and puts a hand out to touch the necklace where it sits just below my throat.

"It looks old," she says. "Where did you get it?"

She's standing so close to me that her body almost touches mine.

"We found it in my grandmother's things when she died. She did a lot of traveling in Asia. I'm not exactly sure where she got it."

"Hmm." She lifts her eyes to meet mine. "Beautiful."

I have never had a conversation with Bianca that has lasted this long. I have never had a compliment from her. It feels good. Too good. And then it's over.

"Well, we'll see you there," she says, stepping back. "Alana? Kelly?"

She marches out flanked by the other two.

Most people who are coming straight from work fit into Bianca's and Kathy's cars, but Chris decrees that he, Ed and I will take the bus.

"But then we'll all get there before Ed," Kathy points out.

Chris turns to Ed. "Give her your keys."

Ed digs in his pants pocket. He comes out with a set of keys on a bottle-opener key ring.

"Eighteen Keith Street," he says, giving them to Kathy.

We all pour out of the staff exit. Ed, Chris and I walk up to the bus stop, which happens to be outside a liquor store. Chris checks the timetable before he and Ed disappear inside. Five minutes later, Ed emerges carrying a case of beer on his shoulder, and Chris carries several bottles in paper bags.

"Ready to party, Youngster?"

Ed looks at me out of glassy eyes, with something that could pass for sympathy. I rummage in my bag for bus fare.

Ed's family lives in a little bungalow on a quiet street. It's very different from Bianca's parents' harbor view, which possibly accounts for how badly behaved everyone at this party is from the get-go. Because it's a small house, everyone congregates in the living room and the small adjoining kitchen.

All signs of Bianca's earlier friendliness have vanished and she sits close to Alana, Kelly, Street Cred Donna and Jeremy. A little later on she sits on Jeremy's knee. Jeremy looks smug. I think Bianca and Andy have broken up—he's not at the party. Kathy seems to be hovering close to Chris.

There is plenty of alcohol and not much food. I nibble at some chips and sip a beer. I talk a bit to Sveta, who is in the same grade as me. Bianca drinks bourbon and Coke, while Kathy has brought her own supply of wine coolers. Several bottles of spirits and various soft drinks are lined up on the kitchen table.

Chris, however, is steadily swigging straight from his own personal bottle of vodka. Full-sized. I'm no expert, but I know from my parents' example that spirits are generally consumed in small quantities from a glass and more often than not are mixed with something else. Chris catches me staring.

"Want to try, Youngster?" he asks.

"Sure."

I put my beer down and bravely grasp the vodka bottle with one hand on the neck and one on the base. I tilt it back into my mouth. The only thing worse than the explosion of foul taste is the harsh burning sensation all the way down my esophagus. I cough and splutter. Chris pounds my back.

"It burns," I gasp.

"Not after a while," he assures me, reclaiming the bottle and taking a generous slug for himself.

After a couple of hours there is talk of playing Twister. Unfamiliar music is blaring. Ed, Lincoln and Vic return from the garage with red eyes. Chris is about halfway down his bottle. Alana and Kelly start working the room with a bottle of tequila and a bottle of lime juice, dispensing something called laybacks.

Observation reveals that this involves lying down on your back so Alana and Kelly can pour tequila and lime into your mouth. It's Chris's turn. We are sitting on the couch and he obediently stretches out along its length, his legs across mine. He swallows his huge mouthful without flinching and returns to a sitting position. Cries of "Amelia!" go up, and I realize it's my turn.

"Yeah, maybe not for me . . . ," I wheedle, the taste of Chris's vodka still fouling my mouth. But the cries become louder and I find my shoulders being pushed back by Ed and Lincoln. I open my mouth as the giggling faces of Alana and Kelly loom over me. Pour! Are they emptying the bottles into my mouth? Undiluted lime juice and brutal tequila fill my mouth to capacity and I wonder how I will manage to swallow it all. I jackknife away from the stream before they finish pouring, splashes of both ending up on my neck and T-shirt. I swallow the whole lot, battling my gag reflex. Fearing I'm going to lose the battle, I struggle to my feet and find my way out to the only bathroom.

I shut the door behind me and take a few deep breaths. I splash water on my face and neck, drying off with what I hope is a cleanish towel. I wet one corner of it and dab at the sticky patch on my T-shirt. Then I sit down on the tiles with my back against the bath. There's a bang at the door.

"Amelia! Are you all right?"

Before I can answer, the door opens and Chris comes crashing through, clutching the neck of his vodka bottle with one hand. He regards me for a second, then pulls the door shut behind him and slumps down on the tiles beside me.

"Not feeling too good?" he asks.

"I'm all right now. Reckon I'll go home soon. How're you feeling?" I gesture to the bottle.

"Me? Fan-fuckin'-tastic. You can't drown 'em . . . but you can make 'em swim for it."

"Drown who?"

"Ah . . . nothing."

We sit in silence. There are some cleaning products stashed under the sink adjacent to where we sit. I spy one of a new line of sponges that I had seen an ad for yesterday and been outraged by. I pick it up.

"Have you seen the ad for the new Wonder Sponge?" I ask. "It's a bloody disgrace. There is some Guy Smiley type interviewing various women—*all* women!—about how fantastic the new sponge is, and how it totally meets their cleaning needs. Goodbye, bathroom tile grime! The women are all very, *very* excited about their new sponge. They're standing in their sparkling shower recesses looking wholesome. 'It just wipes right off!' Guess what? Not a single man! What are we to learn here—that bathroom grime is a woman's lot?" I pause for breath, and deflate. "I guess bathroom grime is a woman's lot. It certainly is in my house." I turn to face him. "Do you concern yourself with bathroom grime at your house?"

He shakes his head slowly.

"Didn't think so." I throw the sponge against the wall in disgust.

"Amelia," Chris says.

"Yeah."

"If you were two years older, I'd be going out with you."

What? What did he just say? I stare at him.

He looks at me tenderly with unsteady, bloodshot eyes.

"You what?"

"I wish you were older," he says. "You'd be the Perfect Woman." And he cups my face with his non-vodka-holding hand.

I'm speechless. I have no speech. All I have is the sound of my own blood thudding through my ears. I don't think I'm breathing. Then all of a sudden I find my voice.

"You are perfect! You are *perfect!*"

"Is that right?" he says, putting his vodka bottle down on the tiles.

"Yesss!"

He cups my face with both hands.

Holy shit.

"Amelia."

"Yeah."

"I'm going to have to kiss you now." And he pulls my tequila-and-lime-flavored mouth over to his.

I kiss Chris as if I've been kissing boys in bathrooms for years. I think I can feel the particles in our lips merging. The inches of bathroom tile between us disappear in a tangle of arms and legs.

"Chris." I extricate my mouth for a second.

"Mmm."

"I love you."

He opens his eyes. His grip on me seems to loosen. He looks frozen. Not the effect I was hoping for. I press on.

"I'll be sixteen in a few months."

He loosens his grip even further. I try to kiss him again, but he moves his head to one side.

"What? What is it?"

There's a loud banging on the door.

"Shit!" says Chris, backing away. He knocks over the vodka bottle, which hits the tiles with a crash but doesn't shatter.

"Hurry the fuck up in there!" Bianca yells shrilly. Several more bangs on the door. Amazing. She'll probably show up to ruin my wedding day.

Things happen pretty fast after that.

Chris opens the bathroom door.

"About time!" bitches Bianca, who is waiting out in the hallway with Alana and Donna behind her, as usual. "I've been—" She sees me standing behind Chris and shoots up one eyebrow.

He grabs my wrist and steers me out. "Shut up," he says to Bianca, who had opened her mouth to say something.

"Chris," I whisper, following him up the hallway. "What—"

"There you are, Amelia!" It's Sveta, who lives near me and had offered me a ride home. "My dad's outside; you still want a lift?"

"Oh—yeah, thanks. I'll be right out." It will be hard for me to get home otherwise. Sunday night bus schedule in suburbia and all. We don't do pickups in my family.

Sveta nods and disappears.

I tug on Chris's hand. "I'm going now."

He looks back at me. "I'll walk you out."

I find my backpack and together we go out the side door into the dark driveway. Sveta's dad's headlights are visible down the end but do not shine on us.

"Youngster," he says, and hugs me tightly.

"I better go," I say, breaking the embrace but keeping my arms loosely around him, conscious of keeping Sveta's dad waiting.

He studies me for a moment. Right up close.

"Your pupils are huge," he says, with the slightest of staggers.

I kiss him once more on the lips. Just like that. Just because I want to. I am astounded at the liberties it appears I can now take, and walk down the driveway with confident steps.

I don't study or sleep when I get home to a quiet house at about midnight. I sit on my bed until about one. Then I change into my pj's and sit on my bed until about four. Then I lie back and doze.

When I wake to the alarm at six-thirty, I fear that I dreamed the whole thing. I've had similar dreams before. My eyes arrive at the pile of clothing on the floor. I pick up my blue T-shirt and inspect the stain on the neckline and shoulder. I sniff it—lime juice. I smile so hard that tears come into my eyes.

Bubble Girl

Meandering home from the bus stop after school, my head lolls from one side to the other, my eyelids droop, but my mouth perpetually curves upward. I try to recall the day that just passed. When Jess refused to get up and dressed, I left her there, left her for someone else to deal with. I don't remember making Mum tea or toast for breakfast. I don't remember having feelings one way or another about my father's directive that I—who had to leave for school in a few minutes—vacate the kitchen space until he—who had nowhere to be at any particular time—finished making his tea, as I was "in his way."

I blurted out the glorious story to Penny before roll call. I don't remember feeling angry when Scott and company arrived at lunch. I'm pretty sure I did badly on the history test, but I haven't really thought about it since.

I am completely focused on the phone call from Chris that is surely coming this evening. What will be said? What do couples talk to each other about? I'll tell him about my day; he'll tell me about his. I'll tell him I love him; he'll tell me the same. I'll tell him I have longed for this day; he'll tell me the same. When am I seeing you? he'll say. We'll arrange to have dinner after work on Wednesday night. We'll go to Rino's again, but this time he'll sit close to me and hold my hand under the table. After dinner he'll walk me home with his arm around me.

My family sits down to dinner at seven-thirty. He hasn't rung yet. He'll ring when he's had his dinner.

"How was the party last night?" Mum asks.

"Fine. Good."

We eat in silence.

"Is everything all right, Amelia?" Mum again.

"Yes!"

When the meal is finished, Mum and Dad light up their after-dinner cigarettes. I clear the table, scrape the dishes, rinse them and stack them on the sink edge. Dad is supposed to load the dishwasher when he is home. I take the phone from its cradle and check the dial tone. I retire with it to my room and sit cross-legged on my bed.

It's nine-thirty and still nothing. Maybe he's watching *Media Watch*. What time is *Media Watch* on? He might think that it's too late to call me now.

After much deliberation, and with the beginnings of panic creeping into my throat, I snatch the phone up and dial his number.

"Robyn Harvey speaking," says a woman who I guess is Chris's mum.

"Can I speak to Chris, please."

"Just a moment, love." She sounds kind. "Chris!" she calls. "Phone for you."

Muffled footsteps and then Chris's voice. "Hello."

My chest tightens.

"It's Amelia."

"Hi."

He sounds . . . what? Dismayed? Gruff? Surprised? Annoyed?

"How are you?" I venture.

"I have the mother of all hangovers."

"Oh, that's no goo—"

"Can I call you back?"

"Huh?"

"Can I call you back, Amelia?" He sounds impatient. "In ten minutes?"

"Sure."

And he hangs up.

I look at the alarm clock. 9:34 p.m. I wait.

There's a knock on my bedroom door. I jump out of my skin.

"Yes!"

Mum opens the door but doesn't enter.

"I'm going to bed now," she says.

"Okay," I say, with a touch of irritation. Why is she telling me this tonight? Usually she just goes without saying anything, making me wonder whether I should take the initiative and go into her room to kiss her good night. But whenever I do, I'm just confronted by her tired face.

Now she stands there, observing me sitting on my bed with the phone in my lap. Her eyes move to my unpacked schoolbag, my desk devoid of books and my desk lamp off.

"Is everything all right?" she asks again.

"Yes!" For one terrifying second I think I might cry. "I'll see you in the morning, Mum."

9:45.

9:50.

9:55.

I jump when the phone finally rings, and pick it up quickly.

"It's me," he says tonelessly.

"Hi." I grit my teeth against the havoc taking over my central nervous system.

"I'm not usually a fan of cliché," he begins, "but I'm going to have to open with 'About last night.'"

I exhale a faint giggle and wait for him to continue.

"As you would be aware, I was drinking heavily last night, which led to me becoming disinhibited and losing control of my actions." He sounds as if he is reading from a prepared speech. After a few moments I realize he is.

"I apologize for coming on to you the way I did," he continues.

"You didn't—"

"But I'm sure you know there is no question of us having an ongoing romantic relationship."

There it is. My eyes fill with tears. I'm afraid to speak lest my voice betray them.

"Why?" I manage to squeeze out.

"Because you are fifteen and I'm twenty-two, we have nothing in common socially and are at completely different stages in our lives."

I know he knows I'm crying. He can probably hear my efforts to stifle it.

"You couldn't participate in my life. I couldn't participate in yours. It wouldn't work. I need someone who can come to the pub with me and my mates, who can go away with me for weekends, who I can introduce to my family and, to be frank, someone I can have sex with."

"I'd have sex with you!"

"Don't!" he says sharply. "Don't even say that."

Tears roll down my cheeks.

"I'm sorry about all this. You were drinking too. It was just one of those things." He must realize how lame that sounds. "I'll see you at work. Bye."

He hangs up.

I lie down on my pillow and let out all the sobs I'd been keeping in my throat.

Ugly

The next morning I lie in bed after the alarm sounds. My eyes are sore and caked in gunk. I suppose I'd better go to school, I think. Mum, Jess and Dad have already left. Mum had to drop Dad at the airport early. He's teaching a few classes at the University of New England this week. Modern Drama something or other.

I iron my school shirt in the kitchen and manage a few sips of tea. I leave much later than usual and the buses are full and much slower. I slink into roll call late. Mrs. Chambers doesn't say anything but marks my name off on the roll. I'm never late.

Penny catches up with me at our lockers shortly after recess bell.

"What's wrong?" she says.

"Chris."

"What now?"

"He said it's all off. He says he was just drunk. He says it'll never... We'll never... He never... He read all the reasons why not from a piece of paper."

"Oh, sweetie. What a gyp."

I slam my locker door shut. "Yeah."

We walk outside into the sunshine and head down to join our group on the grass.

"Are we good for Saturday?" I ask. "I'm going to need some serious chocolate therapy. I might even need you to dye my hair for me." Our usual fallback Saturday ritual is going to the movies, sharing a bucket of popcorn and then sleeping over at either one's house, watching movies and eating chocolate late into the night.

"I can't this week."

"What? Why?"

"I've got a thing."

"A family thing?"

"No."

"What?"

"I'm going to the end-of-season party," she says, trying hard to sound casual.

Every year on the Saturday that the First XV rugby team at the boys' school plays the last game of the season, there's a huge party at one of the players' houses. It's strictly invitation-only and attended by the coolest, sportiest boys and the best-looking, most up-for-it selection of girls. I'm gobsmacked—half wildly curious about how Penny had managed to get invited, half jealous and miffed.

"How?" I stop walking, which forces her to stop too.

"Scott's sister is a senior. She goes out with one of the guys on the team. She got Scott and some of his friends invited—including me."

"You're going with Scott, then."

"Well, sort of. His sister's driving and I'm going with them."

"But they're a bunch of wankers, remember? The alpha males and the female prizes for their achievements?"

Penny says nothing.

I wait for her to make some reference to me going too. She remains silent.

"What if I wanted to come too?" I ask pointedly.

"There's . . . there's no more room in the car," she says lamely.

"No more room in the car," I repeat. "Well, fuck you then!"

The day passes without further incident. At lunch I sit quietly among my group, saying nothing to Penny or anybody and pretending to study for a test.

I don't cry.

In double English we watch One Flew Over the Cuckoo's Nest. Sitting at one of the desks in the back row, I put my head down on my arms and study the grainy wooden veneer of the desk, which is an inch from my eyes. I doze fitfully.

Mrs. Cumming doesn't say anything, but I catch her looking at me when I wake.

The bus trip home is the usual assault on my senses. Three alpha-male rugby players torture a tiny nerdy-looking seventh-grade boy. He fights back, the brave little soul.

I meander home from the bus stop, not due back at work until the following night.

When I get home, Mum is about to head out the door. She says she's going to a superannuation seminar at her school.

"There's a barbecued chicken in the fridge for you and Jess, and stuff for salad. Get her into the bath before six."

The front door slams behind her and I stand in the middle of the kitchen. I can hear Jess watching Sesame Street in the living room. I put my bag down on one of the chairs around the kitchen table. There's a paralyzing ache somewhere in my chest, but no sign of tears. I realize I haven't eaten all day.

"Melia!" calls Jess. "Can I have some Ovaltine?"

Little madam doesn't even say please, I think.

"Can I have some Ovaltine what?" I shout back.

"Pleeeease!"

"Little madam," I mutter, and make the Ovaltine.

At five o'clock she wanders into the kitchen, where I am sitting at the table in front of an empty tea mug.

"TV's finished," she says leadingly.

"Mmmmm."

"Can you play with me?"

"No."

"Ohhwwwwwuh."

"Go and find something to play with for a little while and then it'll be bath time, then dinnertime."

"There's nothing to play with," she sulks.

And then I just lose it.

"DON'T WHINE, JESSICA!" I shout.

Her little eyes widen.

"JUST LEAVE ME ALONE! GET AWAY FROM ME! GO AWAY!" My voice cracks at the end of the outburst. I fling my head down on my arms where they are resting on the table and wail. I feel her little hand on my arm.

"Melia . . ."

"GO AWAY!" I scream into the table.

Little footsteps sprint away, up the stairs and into her room above, where the door slams.

I cry and cry, until my shirtsleeves are sodden and my body exhausted. I hear little sobs coming from the room above me. I get up, blow my nose and splash some water on my face at the kitchen sink. I take several deep breaths. Then I climb the stairs and knock on Jess's bedroom door.

"Jess."

I open the door. She's sitting on her bed with one arm holding Prize Teddy, who does indeed look fetching with his new Nanna-knitted scarf. I sit down beside her.

"I'm sorry I yelled at you."

She's silent.

"I'm *really* sorry I yelled at you." My voice quavers. "I'm upset today."

"Why?"

"A boy at my work is being mean to me."

"Like Felix?"

Felix is a boy at Jess's preschool who often pushes her over in the sandpit. I've threatened to go to her preschool and show this Felix the back of my hand, but Mum always tells me not to talk like that.

"Sort of."

She nods. I hold out my arms and she flings herself across the bed and into them. Holding her tight, I breathe in great lungfuls of her skin and hair.

"I'm going to run your bath and make dinner while you're in there."

Jess has long baths, where she plays out all sorts of dramas with her duckies and various unfortunate-looking Barbie dolls. Crystal Barbie, once resplendent in her polyester ball gown and tiara, is now naked and sporting a crew cut.

Jess nods and pulls off her socks. I wouldn't stoop so low as to ask her not to tell, but I hope that she won't mention my episode to Mum.

Half an hour later we are seated side by side in front of the television, watching one of Jess's shows and eating cold chicken and salad. The phone rings. It's Penny.

Being mad at Penny is not sustainable. She is the reason I don't feel alone in the world. We've been friends since seventh grade and best friends since eighth grade. Penny is my most intimate relationship and I don't know how to position myself in the universe without her by my side. If not for her, I would be some

Holden Caulfield–style loner, alienated and miserable. I'm mad as hell, and taken aback that she is going to this party without me, but I can't stay angry at her. The Chris stuff is unbearable enough; I need Penny. I need to beat a retreat back to our safe harbor.

"Have you calmed down yet?" she asks.

"Only just."

"My dad wants to split up with my mum," she says dully.

"Shit! Why?"

"I don't know. She can be pretty hard work sometimes."

"I guess. Did you overhear them talking about it?"

"No, he told me about it in the car on the way to school today."

"Has he told *her*?"

She was silent for a moment. "No. Not yet. And it's bad timing, with Jamie just home from Banksia House."

"Do you reckon he's serious?"

"Seems to be."

"Where would he go?"

"I don't know, Amelia!"

I can't believe this. Penny's mum and dad are like . . . I can't believe this.

"Sweetie, I'm so sorry. I don't get it. Your parents are . . . You know, they seemed . . . didn't they?"

"Hmh."

"Do you want to come and stay here for a while?"

"No, I'd better . . . no. But thanks."

Radio Silence

When I get to work the next day, Chris is standing at the service desk looking at the roster. Bianca and Jeremy see me before he does.

"Hi," I say, slotting myself in beside him.

He looks at me briefly. "Hi," he says, then passes me the roster and walks rapidly away. Bianca and Jeremy snicker, or I imagine they do. She's put me way up on register sixteen again.

Not a word or a gesture all shift.

Bianca takes Chris off register at about seven-thirty to collect trolleys. He walks past me several times and doesn't even make eye contact.

Jeremy and Bianca seem to be conferring down at the service desk, and then Jeremy is dispatched to my register, ostensibly to take a change order.

"What's happening with you and Harvey?" he asks, as if it is his right to ask such things.

"Nothing," I reply, cursing myself for even giving him that much.

"He ignoring you or what?"

"He's not ignoring me!" Unbelievable! This guy hasn't spoken to me in over three months and now he thinks he can show up and question me about the sorest of sore points. They can sniff out a weak spot, Bianca and her minions, that's for sure.

I slap my change order down on the conveyor belt. He pockets it and raises his eyebrows, then saunters back down to Bianca. Does he ever actually serve customers? I think as a customer with a loaded cart approaches my register.

Surely Chris will say something to me before the shift is over. He has never, ever not spoken to me at work. He'll come and talk to me and demonstrate to the minions that I am still his favorite youngster and the minions will have to quit—or at least reduce—their snickering. Nine o'clock approaches. Everybody starts cashing up.

Chris and I usually walk to the back office together to hand in our cash drawers. Before I have finished counting the money in my drawer, I see Chris yank his drawer out and disappear around to the back office with it. I follow as soon as I can, feeling minion eyes upon me, only to see him bolting out of the staff exit. I stop in my tracks. Ed overtakes me, carrying his own cash drawer.

"Ed!" There's a desperate tone in my voice that even a stoner can pick up on and wish himself elsewhere.

"Yeah?"

"Chris . . . Is Chris not talking to me or something?"

"I dunno, Amelia. Sorry."

He continues on. I slowly put one foot in front of the other until I hand in my drawer. I collect my backpack from my locker and head to the staff exit. Outside, Bianca, Jeremy, Donna and Alana are lined up against the wall, taking drags on their cigarettes.

Bianca looks at me with a satisfied expression. Satisfied that I have been put in my place at last. No more swanning around thinking I'm smarter than them and riding on Chris's coattails. She'd have been dripping with saccharine, though, if it had gone the other way and I had emerged as Chris's girlfriend.

The others don't look at me, but I see smirks through the smoke. They don't say goodbye and neither do I.

On my way home I walk past the pub and see Chris sitting

alone at a table with a beer, waiting for the others to join him. I stop to torture myself with a good long stare. Then I walk home. Tonight, walking alone through the dark streets is frightening. The wind whistles through the power poles and makes shop signs rattle against their fastenings. Once I am past the main roads, I walk in the middle of the street to avoid whatever might be lurking in the shadowy sidewalks.

Getting the Hell Out of Here

Two weeks to the day pass since Ed's party. Work sucks. To make the whole Land of Dreams thing seem worthwhile, I blow my savings on two new pairs of jeans, several new T-shirts and a new pair of Converse All Stars. Blue. One of the T-shirts is cream-colored with brown edging. It has the words CAN SOMEBODY PLEASE HELP ME? written across the front in small lettering.

Chris has continued to ignore my existence. Well, not exactly, but he makes swift maneuvers to avoid situations where he might have to look at me or talk to me. If such a situation becomes un-avoidable, I get the curtest of nods.

I miss him like hell and often have sudden recall of cool bathroom tiles and the taste of lime and tequila.

Street Cred Donna hangs around him a lot, retying the long purple laces on her steel-capped boots. They all go off to the pub together after work. I hover around in the locker room until they've gone so I won't have to parade myself past them all mill-ing around the staff exit. Behold the Dumped. The Publicly Dumped. The Embodiment of Dashed Hopes. The Uninvited.

"I wonder if he ever thinks about it," I remark to Penny.

"It doesn't really matter what he *thinks*," she replies, not un-kindly.

We are studying for our final exams, which are in a week. I'm grateful to have something to focus on. Penny's dad has moved out. Her mum is "on the rampage." Her brother, Jamie, is staying in his room a lot and missing a lot of school days.

"Where's he living? Your dad?" I ask.

"Dunno."

"You don't know?"

"None of us know. He says he's 'staying with a colleague,' but he won't say where. Maybe he doesn't want me to know so Mum can't get it out of me."

I'm stumped. I cannot imagine my father doing this. Yelling at me? Yes. Not washing up the pots and pans? Yes. Leaving the family? No.

"He's supposed to be taking Jamie and me out for dinner this Sunday. But he hasn't rung about it or anything."

Penny has been buying her lunch at the canteen lately. No more school lunches packed by her dad. Sometimes you can spend twenty-five minutes in that line, and the lunch period is forty minutes.

It's Sunday night and I'm studying in my room. My first exam is tomorrow. English. They always start with English. My desk is littered with past exam questions. I vaguely register that the phone is ringing.

"Amelia!" my mother calls. "Phone."

I clomp down the stairs to where she stands, extending the phone to me.

"Chris," she says.

I freeze.

She looks at me, and I grab the receiver and scuttle back up the stairs.

"Hello?"

"Youngster."

"Hi."

"How's things?"

Play it cool, Amelia, play it cool. "Why haven't you been talking to me?" Crap.

If Chris is at all fazed by the question, he deals with this by simply not acknowledging it. He mustn't think it worth answering.

"I'm ringing to tell you some news."

"Yeah?" I'm back in my room now.

"Yeah. I'm ... uh ... getting the hell out of here."

"You're what?"

"I'm moving to Japan."

I founder. And collapse on the edge of my bed.

He continues. "I've got this job teaching English in a small town. An industrial town. It's like a night school. During the day I'll do lunchtime classes at a factory."

"For how long?" I manage after a considerable pause.

"My initial contract is for a year. Then I can extend it if I'm having a good time. I've resigned from the Land of Broken Dreams."

"Uh-huh." I'm at a loss for words and in any case need to concentrate on not crying.

"I'm having a thing at my place next Saturday night. A going-away party. I fly out on Sunday night."

"Mmmm." Strangled tones.

"I want you to come. Work people will be there and some of my uni friends."

Silence.

"Can you write down my address?"

I scrabble about under the past exam papers on my desk and find a pen. "Yeah."

"Sixteen Acacia Terrace, Eastlakes."

"Right."

"Well, I'd better go, Youngster," he says briskly. "Got a whole lotta people to call, and then a whole lotta packing to do."

"Bye."

"Bye."

I sit for a moment on my bed and then drop my forehead on my knees and wait for the tears. I don't have to wait long.

My sobs have started to dwindle to sniffling when there is a knock on my door.

"What is it?" I call, using a tone meant to make it clear to the knocker that I did NOT say *come in*.

But the door opens and Mum enters, closing the door behind her.

"I didn't say come in!"

She crosses her arms and stands in front of me.

"What's the matter?"

"Nothing." I gather up the soggy tissues surrounding me on the bed and throw them in the bin. Not all of them make it.

"What is the matter, Amelia?"

I blink at her.

"It's this boy Chris, isn't it? The one from work. What's going on?"

"Nothing."

"Nothing? He rings and suddenly you are in tears the night before your exams."

I pick at the embroidery on my bedspread.

"And not for the first time either," she adds. "He doesn't seem to be a positive presence in your life."

"He's going away" is the only thing I can think of to say. "Overseas. To live."

"Well, good," says Mum.

"It's not good!" I wail.

"It is good, Amelia. There's no sense in hanging around people who make you unhappy again and again."

Oh, that's rich coming from the unhappiest woman in the universe! "Then why do you hang around Dad?" Tears crowd into my eyes again. "And *me*?"

"What?"

"You're unhappy! You're unhappy with Dad, and with your job, and with me, and with everything. Every day you let me know how miserable you are and that somehow you've ended up with this awful life. And I can't do anything about it!"

"Darling—"

"And it is awful that you have to work so hard and that Dad's away a lot and when he's here he doesn't help. I bet he only hangs around because he's got such a sweet deal here."

"Amelia." Mum sits down beside me. "Now just calm down. Calm down." She sighs.

I sniffle and reach for a tissue.

"There *are* things in my life that I'm less than happy about," she allows. "But they're my problems, not yours. And your father and I . . . well, I won't pretend . . ." She looks down at the carpet. "It was clear pretty early on that I wasn't going to have a marriage where the . . . labor was evenly split. He can be a very difficult person to live with. Obviously. But there's no question of his commitment to me . . . or to his children. Or of mine to him and to you girls, even though I get . . . down sometimes. You shouldn't say things like, 'He only hangs around because he's got a good deal.' You shouldn't say that about your father."

"But he makes me so mad! The way he treats you sometimes, the way he treats me."

"He loves you desperately. He'd kill for any one of you girls."

"I don't want him to kill for me. I just wish he'd take his plates to the sink and rinse them. And help you more. What if you weren't here to earn the steady money and cook us dinner every night?"

Mum seems to grimace for a moment and then she says quite firmly, "Don't try to understand other people's marriages, darling, even your parents'. You'll be lucky if you understand your own. The only thing you need to know is that Dad and I love each other, and we love our girls."

"But you're miserable."

"Don't you worry about it."

I'm suddenly exhausted and so is Mum. We say good night and Mum goes next door to check on Jess. I want to ask her to tuck me in and stroke my hair, but I don't. I'm almost sixteen.

Where the Beer Is Cold
and the Women Are Friendly

A couple of days later an actual invitation to Chris's farewell party arrives in the mail. He's gotten around to whipping up a flyer on the computer. There's a picture of a sumo wrestler with Chris's head Photoshopped onto it and a speech bubble saying, *I think I'm turning Japanese.* ... Below this the text reads:

> I am deserting all you bastards for the Land
> of the Rising Sun, and I'm having a BBQ to
> say goodbye. So come on down to the Harvey
> Ranch, where the beer is cold and the women
> are friendly. 16 Acacia Terrace, Eastlakes.
> 5 p.m. onward.
> Poverty-stricken citizens catch the 851
> bus from the city and get off at the corner of
> Gipps and Elizabeth Streets.

He's done a map from the bus stop to his house.

I'm not going. I imagine myself standing awkwardly alone while Chris, the Land of Dreams contingent and his "uni friends" (who sound even more frightening) lounge around Chris's backyard in easy fellowship.

The only thing that had ever made me brave enough to go to the Land of Dreams parties was the knowledge that Chris would look after me. The bathroom incident has screwed everything up. If it hadn't happened, at least we'd still be friends.

His final absence looms large and I have the whole week to

contemplate it. He worked his last shift at the Land of Dreams when I wasn't there. I think about quitting too.

Penny arrives at my house on Saturday afternoon ready to stay over and study for our two remaining exams. I'd offered to go to her place, but she'd said her mother was still "on the rampage." By six my attention is wandering. Penny puts her highlighter down.

"Look, there's still time to go," she says. "I'll go with you if you like. We can get a bus into the city and then transfer to the 851."

I shake my head. "My mum thinks he's a bastard."

"Well ..." Penny looks as if she is restraining herself. "You'll be miserable if you don't get to say goodbye to him. He flies out tomorrow."

"I'll be miserable regardless. He flies out tomorrow."

Penny gets picked up at about ten on Sunday. I put away the foam mattress and roll up the sleeping bag. Grudgingly, I get out of my pajamas and into jeans and one of my new T-shirts. Mum and Dad are in the kitchen, reading the paper over their pot of tea. Classic FM wafts throughout the house. Jess must be pottering in her room.

Despair at the coming day paralyzes me. And so does the thought that my reward for surviving it will be another Chris-less day. And another one after that. *Get your sneakers on and go for a walk*, I tell myself urgently. *Keep moving; don't stand still.*

Our door knocker raps loudly and breaks my paralysis.

"I'll get it!" I shout, thinking Penny must have forgotten something. But as I approach the door, I see through the baubled glass what looks like a delivery guy holding a box of something. I open the door.

It's Chris. Wearing an ancient T-shirt, clutching an old wine box and looking unshowered.

"Where the hell were you last night?" he demands.

"I couldn't come."

"Why? You know I'm leaving today."

"I know you're leaving today," I concur softly.

"You didn't even ring!"

Mum appears in the hallway behind me.

"Who is it, Amelia?" she calls, eyeing the scruffy young man with the box.

"My friend. It's all right."

She hesitates and then goes back out to the kitchen.

"I bet I'm really popular around here," Chris says. There's something in his tone that makes me think he knows how hurtful he's been.

"Mmmm." I can't think of anything to say.

"Listen, Youngster," he says. "Men are bastards. You can't trust any of them. No matter how genuine they seem."

"I'll remember that."

"Do."

I'm crying. Not blubbering and sobbing, but everything inside is pushing its way inexorably out.

"Youngster," he says. "Amelia. It wouldn't have worked."

"You don't know that."

"Really, I do."

"You don't!"

Having been struggling with the box's weight, he lets it down onto the doorstep. It looks to be full of notebooks.

"I brought you something," he says. "Somethings."

"What are they, uni notes?" I sniff.

"They're my diaries. From when I was fifteen until now. Read them. So you know you're not alone."

I gape at him, then down at the box and back up again.

"I want you to look after them. Will you do that for me?"

He's waiting for me to answer.

"Yes." What else can I say?

"You know," he says gently, "you figure quite a bit in the later ones."

I take this in and scuff softly at the box with my shoe.

"I've got to go," he says briskly. "More packing. Take care of yourself, Youngster. I'll send you my address and stuff when I get settled. So we can keep up the letters."

And he kisses me, roughly, malodorously, on the cheek.

A white Commodore sedan, old but well kept, is parked outside our house. He shuts the gate behind him, gets into the car and starts the engine.

"Chris!"

He rolls down the window.

"Yeah?"

"Shave!" I rub my cheek where he kissed it.

"Will do!"

The Commodore pulls out and drives to the top of the street. Its indicator blinks left and then it disappears around the corner.

I look down in disbelief at the haul at my feet. Squatting down, I pick one notebook out at random and leaf through its pages. It's full of Chris's handwriting, and the chill in my heart starts to thaw. This is quite a consolation prize. As far as consolation prizes go. I lever my fingers underneath both ends of the box and struggle to my feet.

"Darling?"

It's my father. The sound of teacups being put down on saucers and chairs scraping back. My father appears in the doorway, and then my mother, both of them having moved through space and across the parenting continuum to voice their concern for their middle daughter, the one in no-man's-land between the trenches of childhood and adulthood.

"Is everything all right?" asks my father.

"Yeah." I smile at them. Weakly, but still a smile. And I take the box up to my room.

The BLACK Notebook

May 2

There were a few more pages left in the purple notebook, but I felt the sudden need to make a clean break. So here we are on the fresh first page of the black notebook. Oh, the possibilities of a blank diary! The purple one has been relegated to the pile with the others, where it collects dust and insects and waits patiently to never be read.

Rohan's coming to town next weekend for his birthday—his parents are throwing a party for him at their place on Saturday night. The upside of that, apart from seeing Ro again and eating his mother's amazing cooking, is that the engineering set will be there. This will most likely include the lovely Stella, who is soon to be a master brewer. There has been no sex for Chris since She's-big-she's-blond, so I am keen to rectify that. Ed makes frequent reference to my "drought." It amazes me that I've never pointed out that his drought is so perpetual as to render it not really a drought but just the climate. He has been continuously stoned since he was sixteen. Alana (one of Bianca's young chums among the checkout staff) has let him know she's interested a few times, but it just doesn't register with him.

It's Dad's birthday this Friday, and he wants to have a family barbecue at our place on Sunday, including, of course, Uncle Jeff and whatever of his progeny can be rounded up. Run, you buggers, run! After Sunday, I'm going to try to avoid Jeff until Christmas. Maybe I'll even find a way to avoid the annual Christmas visit too. Seriously, if I round the driveway and see his car in it, I'll go up to the pub and sit there for a few hours until he's gone. I'm sick of his bullshit. He can't pick at me if I'm not there. No, that wasn't a mistake—Jeff picks *at* me rather than *on* me. Today

I imagined Christmas after Christmas stretching out into the future. More Jeff getting pissy and belligerent and drinking all my father's good beer. Then, as "his generation" is wont to do, getting behind the wheel and driving home.

Oh, I feel fine, he dismisses me or Zoe when we gently inquire if he reckons he is below 0.05, knowing very well that he's drunk over ten full-strength beers over the course of the day.

Limit, what limit? I have no limits. I'm a smug baby boomer! Back in my day there were none of these DUI inconveniences. They just make trouble for people trying to get home; it's a revenue-raising exercise designed to squeeze yet more money out of a man! I'm fine to drive. Anyway, how else am I going to get home?

Zoe and/or I offer to drive him home in Dad's car.

What? he splutters. But then I'd have to get back here tomorrow to pick up my car!

Zoe offers to drive his car for him, and I will follow in Dad's car to take Zoe home again.

Oh, stop fussing. You young people.

The car door slams. Zoe and I send appealing looks in the direction of our parents—won't they intervene? No, it seems they will not. Either they don't feel it's their place, or they secretly support Jeff's right to drive home drunk.

The dark green Lexus spins off and Zoe and I are left standing in the driveway.

"You know," she said last Christmas, "he's got the right to kill himself, I suppose. You reap what you sow. But what pisses me off is the damage he could cause to other people."

I fetched two beers, and we perched together on the bricks of the front fence, watching the dusk fall all around us. It was the first enjoyable moment of the day.

Seriously, missing out on Christmas has got to be at the top of the list of reasons to live overseas for a while.

May 6

Dad's birthday barbecue went much as expected. Uncle Jeff turned up with his daughter Ashley in tow. She's twenty and in her third year of arts/law, but not at my uni. Zoe and I have always regarded her and her siblings warily, as I'm sure they do us. Again Jeff proved that his problem is with me and not "my generation" by not picking at Zoe or Ashley. Just me.

"Saint Christopher!" he boomed, subtle menace lurking behind his bonhomie. "So, what kind of a job are you going to get next year?"

He asked that question knowing and relishing that it is the most frightening question you could ask a sociology student. When I failed to answer immediately, he turned to Dad and said, "What do you reckon, Rob? What's your boy going to do next year?"

Dad too appeared flummoxed—no, *shamed*—but thank God for Zoe, who arrived at that juncture with a fresh round of beers. She must have been listening.

Mum's sister, Sue, showed up with her husband, Stuart, and their eleven-year-old daughter, Brianna. They live somewhere near some hills. Baulkham Hills, Beaumont Hills, something like that. I don't know why, but Sue loves talking to me at these things. She makes a beeline for me every time, announcing to no one in particular that she's "going to talk to Christopher." Sue, bless her soul, has none of Jeff's menace, but she talks *at* you with this incredible pressure, and any attempt to actually contribute to the conversation—that is, to break into her monologue—gets ridden over. I'm not sure if there is such a thing as a Hills accent, but there's something distinctive about the way she talks. It creeps in around the edges. The only example I can think of right now is that instead of saying, "Yesterday the man finally came to fix the washing machine," she says, "Yesterday the man finally come to fix the washing machine."

She told me about the trip to Europe that she and Stuart took Brianna on earlier this year, and also the aggrieved story about one of Brianna's teachers, who, several years ago, told her that Brianna had ADHD. Which she doesn't. I've heard both of these stories before. But I don't mind hearing them again, especially if it gets me out of talking to Uncle Jeff.

Our barbecue is under the carport and a good few yards away from the main hub of the party. I'd thought that manning it might get me off conversation duty for half an hour or so, but oh, how I was wrong. Uncle Jeff saw an opportunity. I was a sitting duck—all alone under the carport, wearing Mum's apron and tending the steaks and sausages.

He swooped, beer in one hand, fold-out chair in the other, and set himself up next to the grill. I was his captive audience for the duration of the barbecuing. There were quite a few orders for well-done too, so I was fucked.

He sat there, happy as a clam, finding fault with my talents (or otherwise) as a barbecue chef. At one point he stood up and without warning poured his beer over all the sizzling steaks, washing away Mum's prized marinade.

"Gives 'em a bit of flavor, eh?"

I stood still and considered my options for response. I said nothing.

I was in the homestretch, transferring the steaks onto a platter and keeping careful note of which ones were rare, medium and well-done, when he came out with what he'd been saving for last:

"So, Chris, you got yourself a girlfriend yet?"

"No, I . . . I don't have a girlfriend."

"Oh well, that's all good. Not all young fellas have girlfriends, you know. And that's all right, nothing wrong with it. Just the way things are, right?"

I stared down at the heavy platter of meat, considering a range of responses to his insinuation that my girlfriendless existence was due to being gay. I looked down the yard at my dad and saw him laughing with Uncle Stuart, Zoe and my mother.

"This round is ready," I said to Uncle Jeff lightly. "Dig in. You gotta be quick around here."

Zoe and I did most of the cleaning up afterward, leaving Mum and Dad to have some downtime. I carted everything in and scraped the dishes. Zoe rinsed them and put them in the dishwasher. She washed up the big platters and salad bowls that wouldn't fit into the dishwasher. I dried them and put them away. When we were finished, I got two beers out of the fridge and we sat down out the back.

"Uncle Jeff reckons I'm gay," I said.

"No, he doesn't. He reckons he can get a rise out of you by implying it. Did he?"

"I ignored him."

"That's so grown-up. You could never have done that a year ago."

"Yeah, well. I didn't want him to have the satisfaction of making me ruin Dad's birthday party. That would just confirm his pet theory that I'm a useless, precocious little bastard. Plus, it's time he learned that the gay thing just isn't the insult it used to be."

We sat in silence for a moment.

"Hey, are you still cut up about What's-her-face?" she asked.

Ever since Michaela pulled my still-beating heart out of my chest à la *Indiana Jones and the Temple of Doom*, Zoe has referred to her only as What's-her-face.

"Um, sometimes," I hedged. "Most of the time. Yes."

"Amazing. It's been over a year."

"Yeah, well. You know my 'passion for unhappiness.' How's What's-his-face?"

Zoe's boyfriend, Terry, is a fellow commerce graduate. She doesn't bring him round much. They both have graduate positions in accounting firms. Whenever I've met him, he's had very little to say. But I know better than to try to understand what attracts people to other people.

"He's good," she said. "Um, hey?"

"Hey?"

She sounded as if she had something to say. God, is she marrying him?

"I'm out."

"You're out? Of where?"

"Of here. I've found a place and I'm moving out soon."

"Shit!"

She's leaving me here! She's leaving me here, the sole loser adult child at 16 Acacia Terrace.

"Don't leave me here!"

"Chris, I'm turning twenty-four next week. It's time. It's beyond time."

I pondered this truth.

"Where?" I asked lamely.

"Leichhardt."

"Who with?"

"Sylvia."

"Have you told Dad?"

"Tomorrow."

It was nearly eleven. We went inside and watched *Star Trek: Voyager*. It was another one where a holodeck program gets out of hand and threatens to overrun the whole ship. Will they never learn?

May 13

I went to Rohan's birthday party last night, then had to drag my sorry arse into the Land of Dreams for four hours this afternoon. I felt so rotten and tired this morning that I was within a hairsbreadth of calling in sick. But if I start calling in sick because I'm hungover, I'll never make it in there at all. Slippery slope. Youngster Amelia was the only one who didn't make a point of telling me I looked like shit.

As for Rohan's party—well, what can I tell you? Oh, I know! He and the lovely Stella are apparently an item. Completing for one Rohan Levinson the trifecta of a house, a job and a girlfriend. I'm happy for him. For both of them. Really.

I'm going to go out on a limb and say that things come pretty easily to Rohan. He's smart and good-looking; he has a well-off family behind him. He's the only and much-cherished son. He did well at uni. He has a good job and a string of pretty girlfriends. And all these things he accepts smoothly, as though they were inalienable rights. If it was me, I'd be like a frumpy girl at the school dance who gets asked to dance by the captain of the football team. Pathetically grateful and not a little bit surprised. I'd be like:

Oh my God! I fill this shirt out nicely. That's so cool! I'm so lucky to have these nice broad shoulders and dark good looks. What? Money for a deposit on a house? Dad! That is the most meaningful and valuable gift; I don't know what to say except thank you so much! That's a huge load off and there is simply no way I could have done it without help. And Stella. Being able to stand here at a party with my arm around you is so special. You're a beautiful and smart girl and I can hardly believe that you are going to let me take your clothes off later tonight! Thank you! That's tremendously exciting.

Anyway, I ate huge amounts of Rohan's mother's burek, drank beer and fell down. I didn't fall down at his parents' place, though; I fell down when we all went into the city afterward. Just like old times—me, Mick, Suze and Rohan. And now Stella.

Right, let's take stock:

Zoe is leaving me to face my pathetic life-stage limbo at Mum and Dad's alone.

The Field is very slim pickings at the moment.

I haven't heard from Michaela since well before I sent the flowers at Christmas. I don't think I ever will. That's a sobering thought. With some chronological distance from the whole thing, I can see that it's likely there will be no further congress between us. Ever. It's not as if there's a chance of running into her around here. I have these weird daytime fantasies of running into her in the street ten years from now. Perhaps I have my firstborn child in tow. Perhaps she has hers. Our partners don't figure in the fantasy, which I have to admit is lifted mainly from the cut scene in Great Expectations where Pip and Estella run into each other in the street years later. Pip has Joe and Biddy's little boy with him and Estella thinks he is actually Pip's child. Pip is working hard and doing well. Generally getting on with his life. Estella looks sad. She is sad. Her life has been pretty shit on account of choosing to marry some violent prick instead of Pip.

In my fantasy, Michaela looks pale and thin and pained to see me—pained because she remembers how amazing we were together and regrets choosing Brad over me. He's turned out to be one of these totally absent husbands. I break off the conversation first, saying I have to go. I'm meeting my again-pregnant wife for lunch. I kiss Michaela chastely on the cheek and walk off holding my little son or daughter by the hand. I don't look back. She looks after us with tears in her eyes, clutching the hand of her own child, for as long as she can see us.

I love this fantasy. I replay it again and again.

June 5, 11 p.m.

Kathy is doing a teaching practicum for the next few months, so she has cut down to one shift a week. Stuart Green has resigned. Bianca says he's got a grown-up job somewhere. Bianca also says he and Kathy are not a happening thing. I honestly don't care. Bianca is making some not-so-subtle attempts to get me together with some of her youngsters at work—particularly Donna and/or Alana. Both are sixteen, but they seem older. I get on fine with them. Let's face it, I can get on fine with most people if I need to.

And I am lonely. Really lonely. Even a girlfriend I don't have any great connection with would be better than no girlfriend at all. And this drought shows no sign of breaking. I have to seriously consider my options.

Then there's Amelia, who I like better than any of the other girls. It's about time I wrote that down. But she is young. I'm going to be twenty-two in a few months. I'm hoping to move into some brave new phase of life after university, and I really can't see myself doing that with a fifteen-year-old in tow. If only she were a few years older. But she ain't.

Bianca is having a select few over to her house this Saturday night—her parents are overseas again. There'll be a lot of alcohol directly sponsored by Bianca's parents, and most likely a lot of white powdered substances indirectly sponsored also by Bianca's parents. I have to say, I do like the idea of doing a line of speed off their $7,000 granite coffee table, looking out over the harbor at the city lights blinking on the skyline.

June 6

Dad is being all stoic about Zoe moving out, but I think he's worried and sad about losing his not-so-little princessa. It's strange, this modern life, where kids stay at home for so long. When Dad was twenty-four, he'd just bought a house, married my mother and knocked her up. Zoe's the same age, but it's a whole different set of markers. I wonder how much of it is due to changes in education funding and living and housing costs. For most Australian students, there's no option but to stay at home while you're studying.

Mum's putting together a couple of crates of cutlery, crockery and linen for Zoe to take with her. She's also bought her a toaster and a kettle, both of which are gleaming in their boxes in the front hallway. I swiped a few clean empty boxes from the back dock at work for her to pack stuff in.

"You realize," I said to Zoe a couple of days ago in a last bid to get her to stay, "that there won't be cold beer in your new place. Unless you buy it."

"Yep," she replied smiling. "My beer in my fridge."

It's time. Bloody oath.

June 10

It's about midday on Sunday. It's the first really cold day. I've not yet surfaced, but Mum and Dad must have rummaged out some of the heaters because the smell of burnt fluff has seeped under my door. I'm loath to get out of bed because (a) it's cold, (b) a Sunday morning (well, afternoon now) spent solely in Mum and Dad's company will reinforce my status as the only child left living at home and (c) I am delicate, hungover and sheepish in the wake of Bianca's party last night.

Zoe moved out on Friday. She's due to come over for dinner tonight. She'll bring Dad's car back and I'll drive her home in it. On Friday, I helped her ferry several carloads of stuff to Leich-hardt and we loaded up the final one at about seven.

Mum and Dad came out to say goodbye. Mum gave her a Tupperware container of Zoe's favorite "Mum dish"—fish curry—and another of rice.

"For dinner," Mum said. "And"—she handed Zoe a plastic colander—"I don't use this one, so you take it."

"Thanks, Mum," said Zoe, stowing them carefully on top of a stack of pillows on the front seat.

"And here," said Dad, "I thought you might like some of this. . . ." He handed her a bottle of Elliot Rocke Shiraz. Zoe's special favorite—but extremely seldom purchased—wine.

"Oh *thanks*, Dad. Yum!" She inspected the label, smiling. "I haven't had this for ages. What a treat. Sylv and I will crack it open tonight."

A pained silence followed.

"Well, I'd better be going," Zoe said. "I'll see you all on Sunday night."

She and I hugged briefly.

"Easy does it, Ripley," she said softly in my ear.

Next she hugged Dad, and then Mum. She and Mum had tears in their eyes.

"Right," she muttered, fingering the car keys. "Bye."

She got into the old white Commodore, started the engine and switched on the lights.

We raised our arms in salute as she pulled out from the curb.

Later—5 p.m.

Oh, all right. Here's why I feel sheepish in the wake of the party last night.

It was, as always, a pleasure to attend Bianca's harborside mansion. Ed and I caught buses over together.

"What about Alana?" I said to him as we jumped off at Rose Bay. Alana is seriously chasing Ed. He shrugged.

We walked in silence. I've wondered lately whether Ed might be gay. I had a sudden rush of courage and faith in our friendship.

"Ed, are you gay?"

He turned to look at me out of his reddened eyes and shook his head.

"What about Donna?" he asked me pointedly.

"Donna!"

"Donna," he said calmly. "She's into you; you must know she's into you."

"I'm not into her," I said. "I'm lonely and I'm horny, but I'm just not that into her."

"She's an attractive girl."

"But is she? Or is it just a lot of jewelry, piercings and attitude?"

Ed shrugged again.

"Your call," he said.

We walked for a while in silence.

"Amelia's not coming tonight, is she?" he said, sly as a swagman's kelpie.

"Amelia? Nah. Bianca wouldn't have invited her."

"She might've if you'd said something."

"I doubt it. She suspects, quite rightly, that the Youngster knows too much."

"Too much about what?"

"About Bianca. That she's a vacuous, parentally funded phony boho who enjoys manipulating youngsters to fuel her own ego."

Ed laughed.

"That's our hostess you're talking about."

"I know. I feel terrible."

"Are you into Amelia?" Ed asked, with the same trying-to-sound-calm tone that I'd used when I asked him if he was gay.

I laughed. "Am I into her?"

"Are you?"

"She's very young."

"Answer the question."

I struggled. I flailed.

"Yes. No! Kind of. In theory, mind."

"Righto."

We turned onto Bianca's street.

Bianca had set Alana and Jeremy to work making cocktails with a huge, gleaming blender. She circled, carrying a large jug of whatever batch they had just made.

I wasted no time getting into a well-lubricated comfort zone. I even had a half-civilized chat with Kathy. She was looking fetching in one of those crossover top things that accentuated her neat collarbone and those perfect breasts that I will never get my hands on.

"How's your practicum going?" I asked.

"Oh, all right. Actually, this is my fourth week, so it's wearing pretty thin," she laughed. "But, you know, all right."

Crikey, I thought. She can't wait to find some financially solvent backer to marry so she doesn't have to work. I reckon she only chose primary school teaching because it's non-threatening, even attractive, to the banker types who want a pretty, low-maintenance wife to run the house, raise the children and please—but not *titillate*—the business associates. Primary school teaching. A *suitable* occupation for a young lady. Just until the babies come, of course. Then it will be all designer strollers, Peter Pan kindergarten, mothers' group in a well-heeled part of town and four-wheel drives for the bumpy road to and from the beach.

"Are you seeing anyone?" she asked sweetly, draining her glass of passion fruit *caipiroska.*

"Little old me?" I replied, without embarrassment. "No. No, I'm not. You?"

"Actually, yeah. I just started seeing a guy from uni. James Lyon. Do you know him?"

James Lyon, James Lyon. Yes, vaguely. He's one of her library-lawn gang. I've met him at the uni bar a few times. He's in his last year studying commerce. Already has a paid internship at a big accounting firm. Very, very tall and alpha-race-looking. He could well be the one! Good luck to 'em. Of course, what really I mean is fuck them both. But I finally feel I am "on the level" with Kathy—with who she is and what she wants. And where a guy like me fits into her worldview, which is nowhere. I could have provided strawberries, poetry and orgasms, but James, on the other hand, will provide a house in Vaucluse and a six-figure salary.

I can see clearly now. Amelia would be proud.

Anyways, the evening progressed and I found myself in the pool room, playing doubles with Ed, Donna and Bianca. We all drank from large glasses of something lethal and red. Ed and I won the first game by one ball. The second game came down to the eight ball and turned into twenty minutes of frustrating stalemate, broken when Ed sank the white after the black. Ed was disgusted with himself and went off to smoke a joint on the balcony. Bianca excused herself to go and check on the alcohol supply, closing the door behind her. Which left me looking at Donna in the dim light of the custom-made lamp hanging over the pool table. She leaned against the table's wooden edge about a yard away from me, with her arms crossed and her pool cue between her thighs.

"Want to take me on?" she said smoothly.

"Sure."

It was somehow understood that I would ferret the balls out from underneath the table and pack them in the triangle while she sat down on the window seat to roll a cigarette.

"You want to break?" I asked her.

"You break," she said, lighting the cigarette with the huge flame from her trademark Zippo.

You know, I thought as she blew a large plume of smoke and flicked the Zippo shut, *I don't much care for smoke.*

"Where'd you get that?" I pointed to the Zippo.

"America. When I was visiting my mother a couple of years back."

I broke, and sank nothing. Donna sank two stripes with powerful shots. Then she tried a softer shot and missed. She wore several chunky pendants around her neck, all on long pieces of black cord or leather, with the metallic features coming to rest at nipple latitude. Before she bent over to take a shot, she'd pull the pendants around to hang behind her shoulder so they wouldn't spill onto the table.

When I stepped up to survey my next move, Donna sat again at the window seat and produced a small and beat-up looking tobacco tin from her pocket. She extracted from it a rectangular hand mirror, a tiny plastic bag of speed and a key card.

"Want a line?"

"Sure."

With a veteran's dexterity she emptied a quantity of the brownish-white crystals onto the mirror and began to chop at them with the key card's edge. She expertly separated them into two neat lines.

I sank two solids while she pulled a ten-dollar bill from the tin and rolled it up tightly.

"You're up," she said. She held the mirror for me in her palm—at about pendant (and hence nipple) height—while I bent down and inhaled one of the lines through the ten-dollar note.

"Ah, *fuck*," I couldn't help but whimper as the harsh chemical burned through the back of my nasal passages. I sniffed several times.

"Stings like a bastard, huh?" said Donna. She pointed at the other line. "That's for you too."

"What about you?"

"I'll cut more."

I tested for my clearest nostril and bent my head again.

I chalked my cue and took two more shots while she cut a couple more lines and hoovered them up herself.

"Your shot," I said.

She picked up her cue and surveyed the table before bending over to take a shot a few inches from where I was standing. I could see a short expanse of pale skin between the waistband of her jeans and the black and white stripes of her top. She missed.

"Damn," she muttered.

I felt invincible as I strode around to the other side of the table. I sank the rest of the solids in quick succession and then, with a satisfying thwack, the eight ball.

"All over, Red Rover," I said suavely, draining the rest of my glass and smiling.

"Sure is." She dumped her cue on the expensive-looking green-felt tabletop. Then she walked around to the other side of the table and did the same to mine.

"That was good . . . um." I motioned to my nostrils. "Good."

"Yeah, it's not bad."

"I'll give you some money."

She's standing rather close, I remember thinking.

Then she grabbed hold of my front jeans pockets, pulled my pelvis in to lock with hers and kissed me with openmouthed, smoke-flavored fervor.

My poor sex-starved body kissed back immediately and responded particularly well to the pressure of her pelvis. Like I've often said, Donna seems sixteen going on thirty-five, which she well and truly confirmed last night. Her hands were all over my crotch in a matter of seconds, rubbing and squeezing.

Chris, I thought weakly somewhere off in the distance, come on man, don't have sex with the sixteen-year-old. You can stop this now.

But then she took hold of my hands and put them inside her top. And then there was no stopping. Once a man gets his hands on a couple of breasts, he's not going to stop himself—at least I wasn't about to. Especially if he's full of amphetamine energy. But when she started undoing the buttons on my fly, I caught her hand.

"What if someone comes?" I whispered.

"That's the whole idea, Chris," she said in a normal speaking voice.

"No," I said, gesturing to the door. "Comes through the door."

"They won't," she said.

In retrospect, I think she and Bianca must have planned the whole thing and Bianca was guarding the door. Donna undid the rest of my buttons with unnerving precision and adjusted my boxer shorts until I sprang out of them. I kissed her again before she lowered herself onto her knees on the expensive creamy carpet. I gripped the edges of the pool table and looked out over the harbor at the bridge lights.

And that's how Donna came to be performing unmentionable acts on me, and then I on her, in the pool room of the harborside mansion until the small hours of the morning.

And now I suspect I might be in a bit of a pickle.

Zoe's here for dinner. I'd better wrap up.

I'm so not hungry.

June 12

I'm pretty sure I don't want to go out with Donna. I'm due at work this afternoon, as is she, so I figure I'd better have a plan of action. Maybe I could talk to her during her dinner break, if I can take mine at the same time. There's another thing: dis one of Bianca's chums and you dis Bianca. I wonder if there will be ramifications. But I'm not afraid of Bianca and she knows it. It does mean, however, that I can't just not speak to Donna ever again the way I did with She's-big-she's-blond Georgia. It'll have to be handled in some way. I'll report back tonight.

11 p.m.

Turns out I didn't need to worry. Perhaps young Donna can sense a "We need to talk" coming from miles away and is particularly good at saving face. Or perhaps I'd wrongly assumed that because she's a youngster, she'd go all gooey and want to walk around holding my hand after Saturday night. Either way, she played it extremely cool.

At the start of the shift she nodded at me as if nothing had happened. I took my dinner break at about eight when I noticed she was taking hers. I found her having a smoke alone outside the staff exit, leaning on the wall. Some people use their dinner breaks to have something to eat. Not Donna.

"Hey," she said.

"Hey," I said. "How's it going?"

"Peachy. You?"

"Yeah, I'm good."

She nodded, tilting her head back and blowing smoke.

"Um, Donna," I said. "About Saturday night—"

"Let's not do that," she said abruptly and without eye contact.

"What?"

"Let's not do 'about Saturday night.' Okay?" She threw her cigarette on the cement and ground it out under her black boot. "See you back in there," she said, and disappeared through the door.

And that was that. What a load off. I picked up her cigarette butt and put it in the bin before going back inside. Amelia's register was closed. I found her in the kitchenette with a cup of tea and a half-eaten granola bar in front of her.

"Where've you been?" she asked, and pushed out the chair opposite with her foot. "Do you know that granola bars are apparently worse for you than chocolate bars? We've been had, Chris, had by the Quaker Oats man. Turns out he's even dodgier than your uncle Jeff."

I sat there until we heard Bianca's voice over the PA system: "Amelia Hayes and Chris Harvey, please return to your registers." She only uses surnames when she's pissed off.

June 17

The Search for the Perfect Woman is not turning out the way I'd imagined. I'm catching myself having to curb drunken impulses to call Amelia from the pub at three in the morning. I wrote a letter to her from a boring lecture the other day. I want to tell her stuff. I look forward to hearing whatever she's got to say. I like helping her with her schoolwork. Her funny little thought processes provide hours of entertainment. There's . . . affection there. I'd rather her company after work than going to the pub with the others. It's the beer I go to the pub for and the silent, routine camaraderie of being around Ed. I don't go to hang out with Bianca et al.

And people are talking. These things don't go unnoticed. There are snickers and raised eyebrows that prompt me to analyze whether there's a sexual component to how I... well, *conceptualize* Amelia. But that's a fraught issue with a youngster, and my analysis never seems to progress.

I'm sick of my life and I'm sure it's getting sick of me. A big change is in order. Let's throw a few ideas on the table.

1. Transfer to Perishables department at work, full-time. Convince Ed to move out with me. Do that for a year and ponder next move, which could include travel, further study, or—gulp—looking for a real job.

2. Transfer to Perishables full-time for six months, bite the bullet and stay at home, save every cent I earn and go traveling for... who knows how long. God, I hunger for a foreign streetscape.

3. Call Michaela and tell her I am ready to be friends. As above, stay at home and work for six months. Find a post-graduate course in Perth, move there and do the friends thing with Michaela until she cracks and wrestles me into bed. Never, ever come back.

4. This one's a bit out there, but I saw an ad in the paper for an adult English school in Japan looking for native-English-speaking university graduates to be teachers. That would certainly be a foreign streetscape.

5. Get together with Amelia. Accompany her to her tenth-grade formal. Fruitlessly try to convince her fam-

ily that I am a perfectly decent chap. Ignore raised eyebrows from family and friends. Content myself with holding hands and kissing. Accompany Amelia on the upcoming round of her friends' sweet-sixteen birthday parties. Attempt to smuggle her into bars for my friends' birthday parties.

I need a drink. Then I need to seriously consider my bedroom ceiling.

Later

Ease down, Ripley! You've blown a transaxle, you're just grinding metal. That's it, ease down.

August 3

The thing about the Youngster is that she makes me think. Example: she's got this flawed but intensely held take on feminism that comes from deep within her fifteen-year-old breast. It involves how women get continuously screwed in the domestic realm—or, as Amelia puts it, "the hard-won right of women to earn money in paid employment, take out the garbage, do the housework, gestate, give birth to the children, nourish the children, care for the children, bear the professional penalties for having the children, take out the garbage again *and* do battle with the local mechanic over the cost of servicing the car."

"You know," I said to her a few weeks ago, "I never really thought about it that way."

"Of course you haven't!" blustered the fifteen-year-old. "Why would you? You've been raised to take your place in the patriarchy!"

"I never!"

"It's a *subtle* process, Chris. You wouldn't even have noticed your own complicity."

"Youngster," I said, "I have studied feminism at university level. I think I'd know if I was complicit with patriarchy."

"All right then," said the little firebrand, "when was the last time you defrosted your fridge, went through it and threw out everything that was no longer usable, put all the stuff you wanted to keep in a cooler while you wiped out all the spillages, crumbs and bits of unidentifiable food, pulled out the crisper drawers and ledges, washed them up in detergent and hot water, dried them and then put everything back?"

Okay, I'll admit she had me on the back foot with that one.

"I've never done that." I'm not even familiar with the task. I've never considered that a fridge would ever need to be cleaned.

"Well, you can bet *any* money that it's your mother that does it. You could bet your own life."

She went on to reel off several other tasks whose existence I'd never even conceived of but the completion of which is integral to a household's functioning. Then she demonstrated that of course my mother did them, as did hers, and my ignorance of their existence was the proof in the pudding of my contribution to patriarchy.

"Well, I mow the lawn," I said, with a touch of attitude.

"And I bet you want kudos for it too, don't you, you bastard! Hats off to you for mowing the bloody lawn every few weeks!"

At this point it's best to back down and try to steer the conversation toward calmer climes. Like me, the Youngster has a vein

that pops out of her forehead when she gets excited, and sometimes I'm afraid it will burst.

But she did get me thinking. So much so that when I got
home, I took out one of my Kate Jennings books. Amelia had
reminded me of a particular passage. It's from a short story, and
the narrator says:

> I am forty years old and women who reach
> that age and are still suspicious of feminism
> have to be wearing blinkers meant for a
> cart-horse. By the time a woman gets to
> Oneida's age, any residual illusions about
> who is running the show and the interests
> they have at heart will have been stripped
> clean away.

I keep encouraging Amelia to read Kate Jennings. Actually I
want to give her a whole reading list. I want to see her learning
and thinking and analyzing. I want to see a more mature analysis
of whether her mother would be any better off as a 1950s house-
wife. I want her to really think about who's in charge and the in-
terests they have at heart. I want to be around for that.

I've just written a whole diary entry about her.

That's true procrastination. I originally sat down to work on
my thesis.

August 25

Not much to report. If I were to take stock, I'd tell you that I'm
spending all day and most of the nights in my room working on

my thesis, due in two weeks. Except when I'm working. I work Tuesdays noon till nine, Thursdays four till nine and Sundays noon till four.

At home I am seldom out of an old pair of black tracksuit pants, my flannel shirt and my slippers. Exercise is my reward—if I have a productive day, I am allowed to go for a walk at about four. I walk along the nature reserve path, breathing in the cool air.

Sometimes I emerge from my room at about ten and have a glass of red wine with Mum. She misses Zoe terribly, but we don't say as much because Zoe's a grown woman and it's a bit silly to moon over an adult child. I miss her too, but I'm trying to see her departure as a motivating factor for me to get my act together and do the same.

These late-night glasses of wine with my mum are something new. They are due to several factors, methinks. Firstly, with all the written work I have due, I am mostly home in the evenings, whereas I used to be out at the pub and not home until Mum was in bed. Secondly, there is the unspoken, but inevitable, approach of the day when I leave home, so we both have a Last Days appreciation of one another's company at the kitchen table late at night. And thirdly, there's the insidious influence of the Youngster.

My conversations with Amelia have sparked off some kind of change in my thinking. For the first time I'm curious about Mum's experiences, along suspiciously Amelia-ish lines. For example, I asked her about when she married Dad—how easy was the transition to living with him? How happy has it been? I asked her about when she had Zoe and me—did she work through her pregnancies? Was she sick? What was the split of domestic labor like with her and Dad? How much did he share responsibilities?

When did she go back to work? How did she manage work along-side having two small children? And when I asked her that, it struck me with full force that I would never, ever ask my dad the same question. Or any guy.

One particular story she told me has stuck in my mind. When I had just turned two and Zoe four, Mum was on unpaid leave from her job as a primary school librarian. She would do a casual day here and there when her sister was able to look after me but was still essentially on maternity leave. One day she received a curt letter from the Department of Education telling her that unless she returned to her position full-time within the month, she would no longer have it and the next posting she was offered could be anywhere in the city. Oh shit, thought Mum. The school she had been working in was in the next suburb—it would be awful to lose that posting. Zoe was already going to preschool nearby three days a week and she loved it. The women who ran it were sympathetic to Mum's plight and made room for Zoe to go five days a week, so that was her taken care of. But I presented a challenge. Zoe's preschool only took kids ages three and four. Mum was loath to put me into day care for five days a week, but there didn't seem to be an alternative.

"My little man," she said in a pained voice, across the table from her Shiraz-sipping adult son. "You and I were inseparable then," she explained. "We had nothing but each other all day most days, with Dad at work and Zoe at preschool. My little man."

She scoured the local day-care centers and found that the task of finding a place that would take a two-year-old for five days a week, on three weeks' notice, was very difficult. Some could offer two days, some three—all useless. Finally she found a council-run day-care center a couple of suburbs over. They could take me immediately. It was a dingy place and had an air of unhappiness about it. But there was no choice.

I remember it. They made me eat boiled spinach for lunch. When it was sleep time, they put us on fold-out beds that were too high for us to get down from without assistance. I remember wetting myself a few times because I couldn't get down when I needed to go to the toilet. Anyway, we both remembered that every morning when she'd take me there, I'd cry and cry and try to stop her from leaving me. I'd run out into the yard and plaster myself against the chicken-wire fence next to the exit walkway, crying and screaming at her to come back.

When she'd come to pick me up in the afternoon, I'd be plastered against the same piece of fence, still crying and looking out for her return. Mum says that leaving me at that place was one of the hardest things she ever had to do. Awful, she said. And your father didn't seem to understand just how awful.

Amelia reckons that these stories are important. Look no further, she says, the answers are in our homes. When I think of "oppression of women," I think of the suffragettes, I think of things in the past or elsewhere, like women being forced to seek back-alley abortions, women being denied entry into universities, women having to obtain their husband's written consent to leave the country, women being hung as witches or sold as sex slaves, women living under sexist, oppressive regimes. I don't need to look so far away. It turns out my mum does defrost and clean the fridge.

I once wrote Amelia a letter and told her that she doesn't have to look very far to see difference—despite the narrative that is spun by the prime minister and co. about how swell everything is. I encouraged her to look close to home.

She's got me doing the same thing, hasn't she?

All of the cleaning-product ads—all of them—feature women. I was watching one tonight for some new variation of surface cleaner ("that can be used on ANY surface, even glass and wood!"). With her kids screaming in the background, our protagonist faced the camera and said something to the effect of "I work full-time. I have three kids. I don't have time to switch between cleaning products!"

Another one for sandwich bags features a professional-looking lady in her kitchen saying she doesn't have time to faff around with cling wrap in the mornings when she's making the school lunches for her tribe.

Where are the husbands? Why is there not a single ad featuring some dude in a suit, or a pair of overalls, saying he's a busy man struggling with the competing demands of work, house-work and looking after the kids—he needs a reliable all-purpose cleaner or a no-fuss sandwich bag?

No wonder the Youngster's all pissed off.

September 12

Trickstered! Deceived!

Mick and Suze. Mick and Suze are together. They've been together for almost a year! And keeping it a secret from their best mates! I don't know if I'm more pissed off at the secrecy or the fact that they've found love while it continues to elude me. All those times—oh, never mind.

I tried to ring Rohan tonight to debrief, but I couldn't get hold of him. He's probably got Stella up visiting. Mick and Suze and Rohan and Stella. That's lovely. Oh, and then there's Chris.

This was not part of the deal! It was me, Mick, Suze and Rohan—four separate entities linking forces to lessen the blow of existence. A safe base to launch from and return to in the event of a critical incident. Bloody couple kingdom now! I bet we'll never go out again—they'll all just want to stay home to cuddle and watch movies. And if we do go out, I won't be able to concentrate because I'll be all like "Oh my God, Mick and Suze!"

I handed my thesis in yesterday, a milestone that was somewhat overshadowed by this revelation. We went out to celebrate and they just came out with it.

Everything is changing so fast. All the mainstays of my life from the last four years are changing. Have already changed. But I'm still here, dammit!

I'm going to ring up that Japanese English school tomorrow.

Fuck everything; I have to get out of here. I have to have something that's mine.

There's almost nothing for me here.

September 18

I'm so fucking lonely.

September 20

I'm holed up trying to write my last essay. Three days in which to do it.

I'm also filling out my application to the Japanese English school.

Mick and Suze are moving in together. They both got the

jobs they wanted. Rohan's moved into his new house in Newcastle. Stella's just got a job up there too.

At least the Land of Broken Dreams mob remains relatively static. Ed's having a birthday party next week.

I'm twenty-two.

September 21

It's sometime close to midnight. I'm in my room with my third giant glass of red wine and I'm just about ready to relay the events of the evening.

Tonight's Friday. Zoe and Terry came around for dinner. Dad fired up the grill and Mum produced steaks long-steeped in her red wine, garlic and honey marinade. Zoe, Terry and I sat silently allied through Dad's interrogation about when they are going to buy real estate. They gave him the usual response about the difficulty in saving the required money for a deposit and then in servicing the mortgage. He said something about needing to make "sacrifices."

After a flicker of anger, we sighed and felt the usual lead weight of hopelessness settle on our shoulders. Terry changed the subject to the Australian Football League Grand Final. When Zoe and Terry left, I scraped the barbecue and wished that daylight saving would come a little sooner. I heard the phone ring. Mum brought it out into the yard.

"It's Michaela," she said.

And indeed it was. Her voice was at once so familiar and so foreign; I struggled to place myself in space and time.

She was cordial, and to my surprise so was I. We talked for a while about safe things until she said quite abruptly, "You must wonder what kind of person could do what I did."

I didn't reply.

"Brad and I had been together since high school. Five years! Five years and a lot of implied commitment. He's sweet and kind. My family adores him; so do my friends. He's got his shit together. He loves me. He let me come to Sydney for six months because I wanted to. Not *let* me come . . . trusted me to come. I couldn't break that trust."

"You *did* break that trust," I couldn't help pointing out.

"Yes, I *know*," she said. "I'm just trying to explain . . . the situation."

I felt sorry for her momentarily, the sucker that I am. No one wants to be a bastard to a decent bloke.

"For the record, I think you'd have debunked me pretty quickly," she said. "If we'd, you know, stayed together. I'm pretty annoying once the honeymoon is over. And has it not struck you in hindsight that there you were falling in love with me 'cause I was apparently so principled and full of the strength of my convictions, when our very relationship was proof that I have no convictions and no principles?"

"Michaela, I'm not sure what you're trying to tell me." *Maybe she's working up to saying sorry*, I thought. But she'd fallen silent.

"Why did you ring me?" I pressed.

"Brad proposed. We're engaged."

Whack! Pow! Bam! Holy horrible punch in the face, Batman!

"That's ridiculous. You're too young to get married," I said weakly. Which was bollocks—I'd marry her tomorrow.

"Not really. I'm twenty-three now; he's twenty-four. We'll have a long engagement. I'll probably be twenty-five before we actually get married. It's not unreasonable."

"No," I managed, "I suppose not."

"A decision had to be made is what I'm saying, Chris. And I made it."

Silence.

"You sure did. So, are you going to tear my other ball off, or will that be all for now?"

You can always count on me to turn civilized proceedings ugly.

"That will be all," she said stonily. "I wanted to tell you how it was."

"Fabulous. Well, thanks for calling—"

"And I only cried the once, you know."

"What?"

"When you sent me those flowers at Christmas, you wrote something about how I used to cry when we made love."

Damn "Romeo and Juliet" song!

"And I'm telling you," she continued. "I only cried once, so let's not get carried away."

And that, as they say, was that.

So let's raise a glass—I'm going to anyway—to Michaela and Brad—wishing them a lifetime of happiness together. And perhaps a pustule-causing disease or two.

I keep thinking I can feel bile rising in my throat. I wash it back down with more red wine. I've emptied Mum's bottle of Bin 555.

September 24, 11:30 p.m.?

Since Friday night, I have been rampaging around like a bull in a china shop. I'm off-kilter. I'm discombobulated. I'm disaffected. My cup runneth over with corrosive acid. The last glimmer of hope for Michaela and me has died. I didn't even realize I had been holding on to it until now.

If I were less preoccupied by the universe's persistent policy of ripping me off, I might feel a shred of guilt about the Youngster. Last night was Ed's birthday party. Although my memories of the evening are hazy at best, I do remember spending most of it with my lips around the neck of a bottle of cheap vodka and also, I'm sorry to say, on Amelia. That's right. I've sunk to a new low of drunkenly sleazing on fifteen-year-olds.

I've been horribly sick today—my last vomit was at four. Thank God my parents weren't around.

Amelia rang just as I was starting to feel human again this evening. It was too much. I let her have it as straight as I could, which was a huge effort in my delicate state. I think she thought that we'd be going steady. I just can't do that. I can't.

Yeah, if I wasn't a black-hearted bastard with sludge in my veins, I'd feel bad.

Must sleep now.

October 5

I'm going to Japan. Strange. Sudden. Unreal. One-year contract to start. I've already signed it. It seems like a big commitment. I asked for six months—in case it's awful—but they said a year or no deal, so I agreed.

I've told Mum and Dad. I'm about to ring Zoe, then Mick, Suze and Rohan. I resigned from the Land of (Broken) Dreams at the end of my shift tonight.

They offered it to me yesterday afternoon and I took the night to think about it. Latish last night I sat down at the kitchen table with Mum. We were finishing off the bottle of red from dinner.

"Mum," I said, "I really need to get away from here. For a while. I've been here for too long. I don't fit anymore."

"Here?" she asked, gesturing to the house. "Or in Sydney?"

"Both."

We were silent for a moment.

"Well," she said slowly, "I guess you've decided then. You're going to Japan."

"Yeah. Yes."

"Yes. Good."

"Except."

"Except what?"

And I didn't even know what I was saying, but I was saying it.

"This girl."

"What girl?"

"My friend Amelia. She's from work. She's special." I clear my throat hard. "To me. And in general. Special."

"Oh," said Mum. "Are you . . . ?"

"She's fifteen."

"Oh!"

"Nearly sixteen."

"Still."

"I know. It wouldn't work."

"Not now."

"It's just . . ."

"It's hard."

"Yeah."

And we drank our wine and I knew I was going.

And I remembered kissing Amelia, even though I'd told myself I didn't.

I leave in two weeks.

I'm skipping out. I'm going to Japan. See you there.

Clear Water
December

Christmas is a week away. Penny and I take the bus down to Bondi Beach on a Friday afternoon. It's hot and there's hardly any surf. Lake Bondi.

We have a marathon swim. Seriously, we are in for about two hours. We can feel our faces and shoulders burning, but cannot extract ourselves from the cool, clear water. We float on our backs; we swim right out to where the waves are breaking and dive down for handfuls of sand; we swim back and forth across the length of the flags; we swim underwater for as long as we can, opening our eyes to the green beyond. We look back at the crowded beach from the deep water.

"We are going to be the first to get eaten," Penny says slyly.

"Don't!" I squeal, and swim back a few yards to be level with another swimmer.

"We"—she swims over to me with clean strokes—"are going to have buff arms."

"Can't believe I'm not tired yet."

"How good is this?"

I start thinking about the realities of another family Christmas. We are buying presents tomorrow after Penny picks me up from my morning shift at Dymocks. After quitting Land of Dreams I got a job as a seasonal staffer at Dymocks Bookstore— hopefully they'll keep me on when school starts up.

"I can't stand the suspense," I remark to Penny. "I need to know if we are going to have Miss McFadden for senior English."

"We'll know soon enough."

"In five weeks' time! What if we don't get her?"

"We might not even be in the same class."

"Don't say that!" I'm horrified at the thought. "I'd rather neither of us gets her than one of us."

"That is so you."

At last we swim to shore and flop on our towels. It's got to be at least five o'clock. Maybe even six. We drink water from formerly frozen bottles and eat the lunch box full of watermelon we brought, now warm from the afternoon sun.

"Heard from your dad this week?" I ask.

"Yeah, I had lunch with him at his work on Tuesday."

"Has he told you where he's living?"

Her face contracts, but only slightly. Only a practiced eye could tell.

"No."

"That's . . ." But I can't find words for what that is. "I'm so sorry, hon."

"Thanks." She looks intently at the horizon, chin up.

"How's your mum doing?"

"She's . . . she's worried she's going to get screwed."

"Financially?"

"Yeah. And also she gave him the best years of her life."

It blows my mind, the conversations that Penny must have with her mother. My family pisses me off sometimes but I can't imagine us not all together. I can't imagine my father . . . ceasing to exist as a part of us. Moving his things out of the house. Not being contactable except through work.

"Heard from Chris lately?" Penny changes the subject.

"Yeah. He rang at, like, three in the morning a few days ago, drunk in some nightclub in Tokyo. Said he misses me but he's 'spanking the J.'"

"Whatting the what?"

"I don't know. I might have misheard him. There was loud techno in the background."

"He sent me a book for Christmas. By Kate Jennings. It's essays. He wrote in the card that not only will I love it, but it fits into an evening bag, and I can take it places, read it on the train."

"You don't have an evening bag."

"No, but I have that little satchel thing that I take when we go out."

"True."

"I could get an evening bag."

"Okay."

"You don't think I could?"

She holds her hands up in an I'm not armed gesture.

I pour water over my sticky hands, and then on Penny's.

"How's the missing?" she asks.

"Pretty bad."

"What a gyp."

"Sure is." I feel deflated just thinking about it. "It's such a long time to wait."

"Wait?"

"Until he comes back. Almost a year. How am I going to manage for a year?"

"Wait? Manage?" Penny slaps my arm with the back of her hand. "You are not waiting. You are not . . . We are not . . . We have plenty to be getting on with."

I'm silent.

"He might not even come back! He might stay. He might go traveling. He might marry a Japanese girl!"

"No!"

"Who knows? And if he does come back, we'll be finished with high school and out and about. We'll be going off to uni . . . and heaps of stuff. And if he wants to hang out with you, you might let him. But you will not be sitting around *waiting*. You will not be on hold. On ice. On . . . anything."

I look at her. Her brown eyes are brilliant in the pink light.

"We have plenty to be getting on with, Amelia."

"We do? Like what?"

"Well, I'm glad you asked. Like, for example, I am going to get you into a dress before the summer is over."

"No, go on."

"I am. Maybe even tonight."

Tonight we are going to the movies with Scott and some of his friends and some other girls from our group. I've made my peace with them. They're actually not bad guys. And I'm a little less bad-tempered these days. Which works out well for everyone.

I know, right here and now in the warm summer air, that I have to accept Chris's absence. That wishing is irrelevant. That a box of diaries and drawer full of letters do not a betrothal make.

"Plenty to be getting on with." I try it out, digging into the sand with my heels.

"Right."

"Plenty!"

I squeeze her hand, she squeezes back and we sit, watching the shadows lengthening on the sand.

Acknowledgments

The author wishes to thank Mara Print, Julia Shearsby and Stephen Mansfield for their exhortations to start writing this novel, and their encouragement to continue.

And Jamie and Margaret. For everything.